"Niccolo, I don't think you've quite understood what's going to happen here," she told him. "You are biologically going to become a father in around eight months' time, yes, but not—not a hands-on father. Not a permanent, day-to-day fixture in this child's life!" she added slightly desperately.

Niccolo shook his head and smiled, seeming totally unconcerned by the vehemence in Dani's announcement. "I think that it is you who does not understand, Daniella," he contradicted her. "The child you are carrying is a D'Alessandro. More than that, as my son or daughter, he or she will be the D'Alessandro heir."

She nodded. "I do understand that, Niccolo—"

"No, you obviously do not." He sat forward to lean across the table, his face only inches from hers now. "As soon as the arrangements can be made, Daniella, you and I will be married," he stated.

CAROLE MORTIMER is one of Harlequin's® most popular and prolific authors. Since her first novel was published in 1979, this British writer has shown no signs of slowing her pace. In fact, she has published more than 140 novels!

Her strong, traditional romances, with their distinct style, brilliantly developed characters and romantic plot twists, have earned her an enthusiastic audience worldwide.

When Carole made her first attempt at writing a novel for Harlequin. The manuscript was far too short and the plotline not up to standard, so I naturally received a rejection slip," she says. "Not taking rejection well, I went off in a sulk for two years before deciding to have another go." Her second manuscript was accepted, beginning a long and fruitful career. She says she has "enjoyed every moment of it!"

Carole lives "in a most beautiful part of Britain" with her husband and children.

"I really do enjoy my writing, and have every intention of continuing to do so for another twenty years!"

Carole now also writes for Harlequin Historical—don't miss any of the fabulous stories in her wonderful Regency series, The Notorious St Claires.

Be sure to read *The Rake's Wicked Proposal* out in November!

THE VENETIAN'S
MIDNIGHT MISTRESS
CAROLE MORTIMER

~ **DARK NIGHTS WITH A BILLIONAIRE** ~

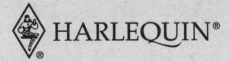

TORONTO • NEW YORK • LONDON
AMSTERDAM • PARIS • SYDNEY • HAMBURG
STOCKHOLM • ATHENS • TOKYO • MILAN • MADRID
PRAGUE • WARSAW • BUDAPEST • AUCKLAND

Recycling programs
for this product may
not exist in your area.

ISBN-13: 978-0-373-52737-3

THE VENETIAN'S MIDNIGHT MISTRESS

First North American Publication 2009.

Copyright © 2008 by Carole Mortimer.

www.eHarlequin.com

Printed in U.S.A.

THE VENETIAN'S
MIDNIGHT MISTRESS

For Peter

PROLOGUE

'So, I've been having wild, orgasmic sex every day with my tennis coach for over a month now.'

'*What?*' Dani gave a start as she stared across the drawing room at her friend Eleni.

The two women were putting the finishing touches to the décor of the country home Eleni would share with Brad following their Christmas wedding in a week's time. As an interior designer, Dani had spent the last month helping Brad and Eleni choose both the furniture and décor for the spacious house that she knew the two hoped would one day be filled with their children.

'Hang on a minute.' Dani's eyes narrowed with suspicion. 'You don't have a tennis coach, Eleni.'

'True.' Eleni, a beautiful Venetian, laughed at Dani's frowning expression. 'But it caught your attention, didn't it?' She smiled wryly. 'I've been talking to you for the last ten minutes, Dani, and I'm pretty sure you haven't heard a word I've said!'

'Sorry, Eleni,' Dani apologised with a grimace.

She had been doing her best, she really had, but obviously Eleni knew her too well to be fooled for a moment. Well, for any longer than ten minutes, anyway.

The two women had first met when they were both fourteen and Eleni had arrived at Dani's boarding school from her home in Venice, sent there for a year by her brother Niccolo, the head of the D'Alessandro family, in order to improve her English. The two girls' friendship had been so strong by the end of that year that when it had been time for Eleni to return home she had pleaded with Niccolo to let her come back to the English school for four more years and complete her education there. A battle she had lost...

Dani gave a shudder just at the memory of her first meeting with Niccolo D'Alessandro, after Eleni had insisted that Niccolo take both girls out to lunch so that she might introduce him to her English friend. Intimidating didn't even begin to describe the arrogantly assured Venetian.

Head of the D'Alessandro banking family for four of his then twenty-seven years, Niccolo D'Alessandro had been imposingly tall, his shoulders wide beneath his tailored suit, his stomach taut, legs long and muscular. Seeing his overlong black hair that he'd brushed back from his aristocratically handsome face, eyes of deep, brooding brown, high cheekbones, a long arrogant nose, a firm mouth that looked as if it rarely smiled, and a hard square jaw, it hadn't been in the least difficult for Dani to imagine that Niccolo D'Alessandro was descended from pirates as well as princes; she had a little more trouble imagining any D'Alessandro male could ever have been a priest, although she had been assured some of them had.

It had been also obvious what Niccolo had thought of Dani after that single meeting—he had flatly refused to let Eleni remain at school in England, only relenting in his decision when Eleni had reached eighteen and wanted to go to university in London.

'Man trouble?' Eleni prompted knowingly now.

Dani shook her head as she dragged her thoughts back from that first meeting with Niccolo D'Alessandro, almost ten years ago now. 'Not in the way you probably think.'

Eleni, her hair darkly luxurious, her brown eyes warm and glowing, shrugged slender shoulders. 'Let me guess. Either you have a man and he's being uncooperative. Or you don't have a man and you want one.'

'I had a man, remember?' Dani pointed out dryly.

Eleni frowned. 'I'm not sure I would call Philip that.'

'I was married to him!'

'Technically, yes.' Her friend nodded. 'But in reality we both know that the two of you didn't even last through the honeymoon.'

To Dani's everlasting mortification.

Philip had looked like a Greek god, and he had been charming, thoughtful, and funny. Until the honeymoon following their lavish wedding, when the jealousy he had been hiding until that point had suddenly reared its ugly head. He had turned into a monster, accusing her of being too friendly with every man she met, from the elderly porter who had delivered their suitcases to their hotel suite, to the waiter who served them dinner on their first evening in Florence.

The scene that had followed in their hotel suite after that last accusation was something that Dani preferred not to even think about!

The two of them had arrived home from the honeymoon separately. Dani had filed for divorce almost immediately, and since that time she had stayed well away from any sort of romantic involvement, no longer trusting her own judgement when it came to men.

'I don't have a man.'

'Then it's about time you did,' Eleni said, having been happily engaged to Brad for the last year. 'Not all men are like Philip, you know—'

'I have no guarantee of that,' Dani interrupted firmly. 'And until I do, I have no intention of getting involved with anyone again. Well…not by choice,' she muttered, sighing as the heavy weight of her earlier distraction came crowding back.

Damn her grandfather, anyway. What person in his right mind would put a clause like that in his will, for goodness' sake? Her grandfather, apparently. If she hadn't complied with the terms of that particular clause by the time her grandfather died, then her parents were going to lose Wiverley Hall, their home in Gloucestershire, where her father had spent years building up the reputation of his stable for training racehorses.

Eleni raised dark brows. 'That last statement sounded very intriguing…?'

Dani gave herself a mental shake. It was a problem, yes, but not an immediate one when her grandfather was still so fit and well.

'Not really,' she dismissed briskly. 'So, tell me how your plans for the reception are progressing? Have you—?'

'Oh, no, you don't, Daniella Bell,' Eleni cut in. 'I'm not

going to be put off by a change of subject. Tell all,' she demanded, her dark brown gaze avid with curiosity.

Dani couldn't help but smile. It was difficult to believe now that Eleni's English had ever been other than what it was. In fact, apart from the darkness of Eleni's colouring, nowadays her friend was almost more English than Dani.

She should never have given Eleni, of all people, even an inkling that something was troubling her. Eleni was like a dog with a bone when she got her teeth into something, and she wouldn't let this go until Dani had 'told all', as she had so succinctly put it.

But maybe she *should* tell Eleni what was worrying her. Eleni was her best friend, after all, and Dani badly needed to talk to someone about her grandfather's will!

She heaved another heavy sigh. 'Do you remember my grandfather Bell?'

'How could I forget him?' Eleni snorted. 'I met him at your wedding, of course, and once before that, when I came to stay for a weekend at your parents' home years ago. But that was certainly enough! He's even more formidably conservative than Niccolo with his "young ladies should be seen and not heard",' she quoted in a fair imitation of Daniel Bell's harsh tones. 'How your poor mother has put up with him living with them all these years I'll never know! I— Oops.' She gave an apologetic grimace. 'I'm sorry, Dani, that was extremely rude of me.'

Dani shook her head. 'The fact that he's my grandfather doesn't make me blind to his faults. He's always been a tyrant and a control freak,' she confirmed disgustedly. 'But the thing is, Eleni, it's actually my parents who have lived with my grandfather all these years. Not the other way around. He owns Wiverley Hall.'

'So that's why your mother has had to put up with him,' her friend realised.

'Yes,' Dani said. 'And my grandfather has never made any secret of the fact that he's disappointed he only had the one grandchild—'

'How could he possibly be disappointed with you? You're gorgeous!' Eleni looked indignant. 'I've always wanted to be a tiny redhead. Do you remember how I dyed my hair red like yours five years ago?' Her giggle was almost girlish. 'I thought Niccolo was going to shave my head and then send me back home on the next plane!'

Dani remembered only too well Niccolo's visit to England five years ago. And the fury in the accusing look he'd shot in her direction when he'd arrived and seen what Eleni had done to her normally rich brown hair…

'And I've always been envious of your amazing green eyes,' Eleni continued longingly. 'Plus, you've become one of the most successful interior designers in London.'

'Mainly due to you and other mutual friends employing me,' Dani pointed out dryly.

'That's irrelevant,' Eleni said firmly. 'Your grandfather should be proud of you and your achievements!'

Dani couldn't help smiling at her friend's chagrin on her behalf. 'The thing is, my mother couldn't have any more children after me, so that pretty well took care of there ever being a male heir.'

'Your grandfather is only a land-owner, for goodness' sake, not nobility!' Eleni scoffed.

And, being descended from nobility herself, Eleni was in a position to know the difference!

Dani smiled wistfully. 'Same thing as far as Grandfather Bell is concerned. "Land is wealth",' she quoted in almost as good an imitation of her grandfather as Eleni's a few minutes ago. 'Anyway, whatever the reason, he's never made any secret of his disappointment that he only has one grandchild—me. When my marriage to Philip ended in divorce, and childless to boot, I thought he was going to have a heart attack!'

'Doesn't he know *why* it ended in divorce?'

'Can you imagine any of the family even attempting to explain Philip's problem to Grandfather Bell?'

Her grandfather was approaching ninety years of age; trying to explain Philip's pathological jealousy, his violent behaviour after he and Dani were married, would probably only result in her grandfather stating that the demand for equality from woman nowadays—that he so disapproved of!—was obviously to blame.

'But the failure of your marriage wasn't your fault, Dani.' Eleni reached out a hand to grasp one of Dani's. 'You do know that, don't you?' She frowned. 'I only ask because I know there hasn't been a single man in your life since that awful marriage.'

'Nor a married one, either!' Dani retorted cheekily.

Although, in all honesty, it wasn't a subject she found in the least amusing. Not when her sex life, or lack of it, was the basis of her current problem!

'Very funny,' her friend drawled sarcastically as she straightened. 'But I still don't see how any of this affects you, Dani.'

In the normal course of events it shouldn't have; when her grandfather died, Dani's father should quite naturally inherit Wiverley Hall and the stables. Except her grandfather had decided otherwise…

'My father will only inherit Wiverley Hall and the Wiverley Stables if I have produced—or at least shown signs of producing—an heir before my grandfather dies.' Dani winced at just putting into words the terms of the clause that her grandfather had recently told her he had added to his will, let alone actually acting on it! 'Otherwise the whole thing is to be sold and the money given to charity.'

Eleni gasped as she sat back in obvious shock. 'But that's—that's positively Machiavellian!'

'Tell me about it,' Dani agreed, relieved to have talked to someone other than her parents about this at last.

Her parents had obviously been distressed a week ago, when Daniel Bell had called them all together to inform them of the changes he had made to his will, but not as shocked as Dani herself.

As Eleni had already pointed out, Dani had stayed well away from becoming involved in any sort of relationship since her ill-fated marriage to Philip, so how she was supposed to produce this heir any time in the near future she had no idea. Solicit some poor unsuspecting man off the street? Pay someone to get her pregnant? The whole thing was ludicrous!

As she might have known they would, her parents had totally dismissed the clause, advising Dani to ignore it too. They'd stated that when the time came they would move the stables elsewhere.

But Dani knew that was easier said than done when her grandfather controlled the purse strings, too.

Eleni gave a dazed shake of her head. 'So is his idea that you get married again?'

'I have no intention of marrying again. You know that,' Dani said.

'But Dani '

'I will never put myself in such a vulnerable position ever again, Eleni,' she stated emphatically. 'Even seeing your own happiness with Brad as an example of how good a relationship can be,' she added tactfully. 'Besides, Grandfather hasn't said I have to actually get married again, only produce the Bell heir.'

'Incredible.' Eleni still looked dazed. 'I thought Niccolo was being unreasonable a year ago when he was so against my wanting to marry an Englishman, but your grandfather's behaviour is positively archaic!'

Dani had been present on the day that Eleni told her brother she intended marrying Brad and living in England with him—moral support, Eleni had called it!—and could clearly remember Niccolo D'Alessandro's icy disapproval that his sister should be contemplating marrying anyone who was not a Venetian.

She also remembered the way Niccolo had looked so coldly down his arrogant nose at her that day, as if he suspected *her* of being responsible for Eleni's stubborn refusal to back down. Not true, of course, but Dani had known there was no point in even trying to defend herself against such prejudice.

As Eleni and Brad's wedding was due to take place next weekend it was obvious who had won that particular battle—and that was yet another thing Niccolo D'Alessandro would no doubt blame Dani for!

'I know that, and you know that, but my grandfather has never claimed to be a reasonable man,' Dani said.

'But—'

'Can we please not talk about this anymore today, Eleni?' Dani cut in. 'I've thought of nothing else for the last week, and it just gives me a headache.'

'I'm not surprised.' Eleni frowned. 'You should have talked to me about it before, Dani,' she admonished her friend. 'I can't believe your mother and father would really lose Wiverley Hall and the stables if you haven't—'

'Eleni, please! Can we talk about your wedding next week instead?' Then Dani shuddered as a thought occurred to her. 'Has Niccolo arrived yet?' she asked tentatively.

Eleni, diverted by Dani's obvious aversion to seeing her brother again, shook her head. 'I've never understood why you and Niccolo have never become friends.'

'Probably because we are both of the opinion that the less we see of each other the better,' Dani retorted.

'But you're the two people I love most in the world—apart from Brad, of course—and I can feel the antagonism start to rise the moment the two of you are in the same room together!' Eleni wailed.

Niccolo D'Alessandro was thirty-seven now, to Dani's almost twenty-four, and the crush Dani had once had on the arrogant Venetian had—as Eleni so rightly pointed out—developed into antagonism on both sides. Out of dislike and disapproval on Niccolo's side—especially after Dani's brief marriage and divorce—and out of pure self-defence on hers.

She gave a dismissive shrug. 'We just don't like each other.'

'But why don't you?' Eleni pressed, frustrated. 'I know I'm his sister, but you have to admit that Niccolo is the epitome of "tall, dark, and handsome", and he has such a dangerous sexual aura about him he should come with a public health warning. And you're absolutely gorgeous—'

'So you already said,' Dani teased. 'None of which alters the fact that your brother makes me break out in a rash every time I see him, and that I seem to have the same effect on him.'

'It's a total mystery to me,' Eleni continued. 'Niccolo is usually so stiffly correct, so—so Venetian, that I simply don't understand his behaviour whenever he's around you.'

Dani chuckled softly. 'One of life's mysteries you're just going to have to live with, I'm afraid.' She glanced at her wristwatch. 'Now, I really will have to go; I have another appointment in town later this morning.'

'But I haven't told you about our plans for the honeymoon yet,' Eleni protested.

'And I would really rather you didn't. Besides, I really don't have any more time.'

'Don't forget we have the final fitting for your bridesmaid's dress in the morning,' her friend reminded her.

'As if!' Dani slung her capacious bag over her shoulder. She was wearing her usual work clothes: fitted black trousers and, today, a cashmere sweater the same deep green as her eyes. 'Although I doubt anyone will even notice what I'm wearing once you appear in that delectable froth of white lace.'

'I have every intention of introducing you to all my eligible male cousins next Saturday, you know,' Eleni promised.

Dani shook her head. 'Introduce away, Eleni, but I can assure you I won't fall for any of them.' Especially if they were anything like the arrogantly forceful Niccolo D'Alessandro!

'Maybe not at the wedding next weekend, but how about at my masquerade party here next summer?'

Dani knew that was part of the reason that Eleni had fallen in love with this particular house. Her friend had taken one look at the spacious garden with its numerous trees and shrubs and instantly decided that the following August she would throw a real Venetian masquerade party there. In fact, her friend was almost as excited about the party next summer as she was about her wedding next week!

'Not then, either,' Dani said dryly.

'But *everyone* falls in love during the Venetian Festival,' her friend protested. 'I remember my Aunt Carlotta telling me that she once spent the whole evening at one of the festivals flirting with her own husband—my Uncle Bartolomeo—without even realising it!'

Dani grinned. 'I bet he was surprised!'

'From the becoming blush on my aunt's cheeks when she told me about it afterwards I would say they both were!'

'Eleni!' Dani chided laughingly.

'You'll see at the party next year,' her friend promised. 'The festival is a way for everyone to misbehave without anyone needing to feel guilty about it.'

'Even your brother?' Dani taunted.

'Well…perhaps not Niccolo,' Eleni conceded. 'But the party is months away, Dani, and if you haven't solved the problem with your grandfather's will by then, an evening of anonymity could be the answer.'

'No, Eleni,' Dani said, easily able to guess what her friend was about to suggest, and having no intention of being seduced into the shrubbery by one of Eleni's male cousins in order to become pregnant. 'I know exactly what you're thinking, and the answer is most definitely no,' she repeated firmly.

'But—'

'*No*, Eleni.'

'It was just an idea.' Her friend shrugged ruefully.

'Well, it was a lousy one—oh!' Having intended making her way out of the house to her car in the driveway, Dani instead found herself crashing painfully into something very hard and unyielding.

A man's chest, she realised, once the pain in her jarred chin had abated to a mild throb.

Niccolo D'Alessandro's chest, Dani discovered breathlessly when she raised her gaze reluctantly to look at his handsome face above a black silk sweater.

Brooding dark eyes chillingly returned her startled gaze, and that same coldness was in the derisive twist of Niccolo's sculptured lips as he grasped the tops of her arms with elegantly long hands and put her firmly away from him.

'Danlella,' he acknowledged as he released her. 'I should have guessed.'

Dani's eyes narrowed at his sarcastic tone. 'Should have guessed what, exactly?' she challenged, two bright wings of colour in her cheeks. Colour she knew would not be complementary to the bright red of her straight below-shoulder-length hair.

But at least she had the answer to her earlier question—Niccolo had obviously arrived in England for the wedding next Saturday.

And he was looking even more devastatingly gorgeous than ever, making Dani's pulse race and her breath catch in her throat. The colour burning her cheeks was from physical awareness this time. Complete physical awareness. Of Niccolo D'Alessandro.

Her breasts tingled uncomfortably and a fierce heat gathered between her thighs.

Oh, God!

She had thought she was over this infatuation—had imagined that no man would appeal to her ever again after what Philip had done to her. But she knew she had been wrong as every nerve ending, every part of her, silently screamed her attraction to Niccolo—of all men!

She looked up at him from beneath lowered dark lashes. Maturity had given him lines beside those chocolate-brown eyes and the firmness of his mouth, but instead of detracting from his good looks they merely added another layer to his attraction, giving him that dangerous sexual aura Eleni had alluded to earlier.

Niccolo was dangerous, Dani acknowledged to herself. He exuded power, a complete domination over everything and everyone within his vicinity.

Well, not her. She'd had enough of domineering men—Philip and her grandfather to name but two—to last her a lifetime.

She turned away abruptly. 'Never mind,' she said, in answer to her own question.

'I thought this morning would be the perfect opportunity for Niccolo to come by and look at the house,' Eleni said awkwardly.

Dani knew by the way Eleni refused to meet her gaze that there was a lot more to it than that. By inviting him here at the same time as Dani, Eleni had perhaps been hoping for yet another chance of reconciling her brother with her best friend.

Dani sighed in irritation. 'I really do have to go now, Eleni.'

'Surely you are not leaving on my account, Daniella?' Niccolo taunted softly, his voice moving like husky velvet across Dani's already sensitised flesh.

Dani's chin rose at the challenge she heard in his tone. 'No, I was leaving anyway,' she snapped.

Niccolo watched Daniella Bell from between narrowed lids, noting that she wore her red hair longer than when he had seen her at Eleni's engagement party a year ago. Now styled in layers, it tumbled fierily onto her shoulders and down her spine. Long, dark lashes were lowered over eyes he knew to be an unfathomable green. Her nose was small and pert and dusted with a dozen or so freckles. Her face was thinner than he remembered, her cheeks hollow, giving those softly pouting lips a fuller appearance above her determinedly pointed chin. Her loss of weight was also borne out by the slenderness of her waist and narrow hips, although her breasts were still firmly full.

And unless he was mistaken—and Niccolo felt sure that he wasn't—they were also naked beneath that clinging green sweater!

His mouth tightened. Ten years ago he had not approved of or understood Eleni's affection and friendship for the gawky English girl she had only known for less than a year, and had absolutely refused to allow his sister to complete her education in England so that she could remain in England with her new friend. Eleni had eventually complied with his decision, of course, and instead continued the friendship by telephone and letter.

Then, at the age of eighteen, a much more stubbornly determined Eleni had informed him that she intended attending an English university, and she had instantly met up with Daniella Bell again. If anything, the friendship between the two women had become all the stronger as they had matured.

Admittedly Daniella had grown into a self-assured woman of passable beauty, and Eleni reported she was very successful as an interior designer, but Niccolo still did not approve of her as a friend for his young sister. Even less so after Daniella's brief marriage two years ago, followed by an equally hasty divorce. It just proved how fickle she really was.

'I'll see you later.' Daniella moved to kiss Eleni on the cheek. 'Mr D'Alessandro.' She gave him a curt nod as she straightened.

Daniella didn't exactly approve of him either, Niccolo recognised with wry self-mockery.

'What? You have no parting kiss for me, Daniella?' he asked, a smile curving his lips as she stared at him incredulously.

'We're hardly kissing acquaintances, Mr D'Alessandro,' she finally managed to splutter in disgust.

'Possibly not.' He drawled his amusement. 'Perhaps when we meet again at the wedding…?'

Those green eyes flashed. 'I believe I will forgo that dubious pleasure!' she came back waspishly.

Niccolo's gaze was intent on Daniella as he ignored his sister's snort of laughter at his expense.

Daniella, he knew, had been in awe of him when they'd first met almost ten years ago—an awe that had quickly turned to infatuation. An infatuation he had been aware of, but had chosen to ignore, even to deliberately rebuff; to a man of twenty-seven years of age Daniella Bell's calf-like devotion as she'd watched his every move with those deep green eyes had been a danger as well as a nuisance.

It was an infatuation she'd seemed to have got over completely by the time the two of them had met again years later, when he'd delivered Eleni to England at the start of the university term.

But Daniella had grown up in the last five years, Niccolo recognised, and in her maturity she was certainly no longer in awe of him.

In fact, it was safe to say that over the last five years Daniella had become less in awe of him than any other person of his acquaintance!

As head of the D'Alessandro family, and of D'Alessandro Banking, Niccolo was accustomed to wielding power and authority, to having his every instruction obeyed. His domestic needs at the D'Alessandro palace—his title of prince had fallen into disuse several centuries ago—were supplied quietly and efficiently, usually before he had even made them known. And no one, in any sphere of his life, stood up to him or answered him back in the frank way that Daniella Bell did on the rare occasions they met.

'The prospect of the two of us ever kissing seems just

as unpleasant to me, I do assure you,' he said, deliberately baiting her.

'Then it's so nice to know we're agreed on something!' Daniella snapped, before turning sharply on her heel and leaving.

'Why do you do that, Niccolo?' Eleni asked gently once the two of them were alone.

He turned to look at his sister. 'Do what?'

'Behave like such a—a—an overbearing Venetian!' she accused.

'But Eleni, I *am* an overbearing Venetian,' he returned mockingly.

'Yes, but you don't have to keep proving it!' His sister glared at him.

Niccolo gave a rueful shake of his head. 'Your friend brings out the worst in me, I am afraid.'

'And you bring out the worst in her!' Eleni muttered with a frown.

Niccolo was unconcerned. 'Then it seems we are all agreed it is best if Daniella and I stay well away from each other.'

'I suppose so,' Eleni conceded heavily, disappointed they both so obviously felt that way.

'Cheer up,' Niccolo teased affectionately. 'After the wedding she and I will probably have no further reason ever to meet again.'

'What about my masquerade party in the summer?' his sister protested. 'The two of you are sure to meet again then.'

Not if Niccolo first ensured that he knew exactly which of Eleni's masked guests was Daniella Bell—and then avoided her like the plague!

CHAPTER ONE

Eight months later...

DANI was feeling hot and bothered by the time she arrived very late—it was well after ten o'clock—to Eleni's masquerade party.

A problem with a client had come up at the last moment, delaying her in getting ready. Then, when the taxi had arrived to drive her here, she'd realised she had another problem. It was an extremely warm evening, and her gown was made out of soft gold and very heavy velvet, and the hoops beneath the skirts kept springing up and almost hitting her in the face.

How on earth, Dani wondered wrathfully, had women ever managed to move around in these clothes two hundred and fifty years ago, let alone eat or drink in them?

Dani gave her cloak to Jamieson the butler after being admitted to the house, before moving to the mirror in the hallway to check her appearance. The gold mask she wore covered her face from brow to top lip, and her red hair was covered with the white powder that had been the fashion of those days. The low neckline of the gold gown showed an expanse of breasts pushed up to a creamy swell by a corset, which also held her waist nipped in tightly, and the full skirt billowed out and over the gold slippers that matched the dress.

Yes, she was as ready as she was ever going to be to face all the other guests, who were already outside in the romantically lit garden.

Eleni had telephoned Dani yesterday so that she could tell her all about her plans for the masquerade party. The garden was to be lit only by lamps and strings of coloured lights in the trees and bushes, with a small orchestra hired to add to the romance of the evening. But even so Dani was totally unprepared for the magical appearance of everything and everyone when she stepped outside on her way to the rose garden where Jamieson had told her Brad and Eleni were greeting their guests.

The costumes of the two hundred or so guests were exquisite, and the masks even more so—a lot of them intricately decorated, especially those worn by Eleni's Venetian relatives—giving Dani a feeling of unreality, as if she really had stepped back into another time.

It was easy to see how and why, with so many corners of the spacious garden left in darkness, those flirtations Eleni had spoken of took place!

Dani quickly made her way to the rose garden, keeping a wary eye out for Eleni's obnoxious brother—a man she thankfully hadn't seen in the eight months since Eleni and Brad's wedding, an occasion when they had all but ignored each other.

'Is that you, Dani?' Eleni greeted her warmly as soon as she saw her, her own Georgian-style costume an elegant red, her mask silver and her dark hair unpowdered.

'You aren't supposed to know it's me.' Dani frowned behind her mask.

'We discussed these dresses once—don't you remember?' her friend said as Dani moved to kiss a Duke-of-Wellington-costumed Brad.

As it happened, Dani did remember the time she and Eleni had lain under an oak tree in the school grounds, waxing lyrical about how romantic it must have been to live in the seventeen hundreds, with all those manly heroes from the historical novels they'd devoured. Until they had remembered that there had been no plumbing for instant hot baths in those times, nor the convenience of the telephone!

But like Eleni, Dani hadn't been able to resist wearing a beautiful gown in the style of that century this evening.

'You both look very beautiful,' Brad told them gallantly.

He was nothing like those dark, almost satanic heroes Dani and Eleni had once drooled over, with his hair a golden blond and his eyes blue, but there was no doubting the happiness of Eleni and Brad's marriage, Dani recognised almost wistfully, as Brad turned to give his wife a lingering kiss.

'Just tell me what Niccolo is wearing so that I can once again avoid him!' Dani begged of her friend as she realised she was holding up the receiving line.

'He's a p—'

'Just think of the D'Alessandro ancestry and you'll know him,' Eleni cut smoothly across Brad. 'And you see all those good-looking men gathered by the bar?' She nodded towards five men laughing and talking together as they sipped champagne. 'D'Alessandros every one,' she said with satisfaction. 'You met them all at the wedding last year, and I'm sure that any one of them would be pleased to oblige you, if you know what I mean…?'

'Very funny.' Dani shot her friend a silencing glare before moving off to join the rest of the guests strolling in the garden, knowing exactly what her friend was referring to even if Brad didn't. In the eight months since she had spoken to Eleni about her grandfather's will, Dani hadn't even come close to finding a solution to that particular problem.

But Eleni was right about the D'Alessandro men all being good-looking, Dani acknowledged ruefully as she stood a short distance away from them. All of them were dark-haired, very tall, with athletically fit bodies. In fact any one of them could be Niccolo, she realised in dismay.

One was dressed as a nobleman. Another as a priest. The third as a gondolier. The fourth was a nineteenth-century Italian soldier. The fifth was in Regency-style clothes.

Exactly what had Eleni meant by her cryptic comment about the D'Alessandro ancestry in reference to Niccolo's costume?

'Champagne…?'

She turned to find a rakish-looking pirate standing at her side—another one of Eleni's D'Alessandro cousins? This man's dark hair was pulled back and tied with a black bow at his nape, and a black mask covered his face from brow to top lip. Tight black trousers were tucked into black boots, emphasising the long length of his legs, a black sash was about his waist, and a long black leather tunic was worn over the white billowy shirt that was *de rigueur* for any respectable pirate.

Except pirates weren't respectable by definition, were they?

This one certainly didn't look as if he was. Dark, dark eyes glittered through the slits in the mask as his gaze roamed boldly over Dani, from her toes to her powdered hair and then back to her face behind the gold mask.

'Champagne...?' he prompted again huskily, and he held out one of the two glasses he held in his hands.

Dani swallowed hard, not taking her gaze off the pirate for even a second. It was one thing to fantasise about meeting a man like this when you were an impressionable teenager. Another thing altogether, at the age of twenty-four, to find yourself face to face with a man who looked as if he were every bit as dangerous as the pirate he was dressed as.

Which meant he *definitely* had to be a D'Alessandro cousin!

Still, it was a masquerade party, where no names were exchanged and there would be no expectations after tonight. Eleni was right; it could be fun for Dani to just anonymously enjoy herself for one evening.

Until ten minutes ago Niccolo had been finding the evening tedious. Conversation became louder as bottles of champagne began to disappear, the laughter too shrill, the flirtations more obvious—and the culmination of those flirtations was obvious as couples began to disappear off into the darkness of the garden.

But Niccolo had never particularly enjoyed the Venetian Festival, and he certainly had no intention of being lured into the privacy of the surrounding trees by any of the women who had so far tried to tempt him.

As usual, he had kept a wary eye out for the sharp-tongued Daniella Bell as each of the female guests had arrived, but at ten o'clock he had assumed that she either wasn't here at all or he had missed her in the crowd.

In fact, until he had seen the woman in the gold gown enter the garden, he had been considering taking a bottle of champagne and disappearing into the relative privacy of Eleni's conservatory.

The woman's hair was powdered white, and she had a heart-shaped beauty mark above her top lip. The creamy swell of her breasts was inviting above the low neckline of the gold gown, and her arms were white and slender, a gold fan held in one of her delicately graceful hands.

Her very stillness made her stand out from the rest of the guests as she looked slowly about her with an almost untouchable air of separation from those about her.

It was a feeling Niccolo easily recognised and related to. As head of the D'Alessandro family and banking consortium he had to keep himself apart out of necessity. The fact that he hadn't yet found a woman suitable to become the D'Alessandro bride only added to his aloofness.

But he put on hold his plan to disappear the moment he saw the woman in the gold gown. Instead he collected two glasses of champagne and made his way determinedly towards her before any of the other men present sensed her air of detachment and saw it as the same challenge he did.

She was even more alluring close up, her skin as pale as milk. The colour of her eyes was not discernible behind the mask in the poorly illuminated garden, but somehow Niccolo thought they would be blue. Her perfect bow of a mouth was highly erotic, with that heart-shaped beauty mark above the fuller top lip, and Niccolo believed the hair beneath the powder would probably be a rich burnished gold.

Dani felt slightly flustered by the intensity of that dark gaze—not sure that encouraging this man by accepting a glass of champagne would be a good idea. Although she had no doubt that the more mischievous Eleni wouldn't have hesitated.

'Thank you.' Her voice was husky as she took the glass of champagne the pirate presented to her, not quite managing to avoid touching the man's long, slender fingers as she did so, and feeling something like an electric jolt up her arm as her own fingers briefly made contact with his.

'Our hostess has strictly forbidden us the use of our own names,' he said with a wicked smile. 'So, if you have no objection, I would like to call you Belladonna.'

His voice was very deep and very sexy. Dani suddenly became aware that she was slowly being seduced.

'As in the poison?' she said pertly.

His teeth gleamed very white in the darkness as he grinned at her appreciatively. 'As in beautiful lady,' he corrected softly. 'And you *are* very beautiful.'

Dani's smile widened at the compliment 'How can you possibly tell?'

'Would you really like me to tell you?'

Slowly being seduced? This man's intent had just gone up a couple of notches!

But it was fun, she realised with dawning wonder. More fun than she'd had in a very long time.

'Yes, please,' she invited.

'You have skin like white satin, a mouth that was surely made for kissing, and breasts—'

'I think perhaps you should stop there!' Had she thought only a couple of notches? Make that a dozen or so! She was starting to feel light-headed from all this flattery, and she had only sipped at the champagne.

'Perhaps for the moment…' He gave in gracefully with an inclination of his head. 'Would you care to dance?'

Would she? The idea certainly had its appeal. But who *was* this man? The dark hair, swarthy skin and slight accent gave no clue other than that he was probably a D'Alessandro relative. What if he should turn out—horror of horrors!—to be Niccolo D'Alessandro himself?

It would be just her luck, when they all removed their masks at midnight, to discover she had spent the evening flirting with Niccolo!

No, she realised with some relief as she glanced briefly across at the other D'Alessandro men. They had just been joined by a sixth man, even taller than they were and dressed very lavishly, and his regal air of arrogance was unmistakably that of Eleni's brother.

Dani relaxed slightly as she turned back to the pirate at her side. 'And what do I call you?'

'What would you like to call me?' he countered.

Dani felt a quiver of excitement down her spine as her body was suffused with a heat that was in no way connected to the warmth of this beautiful summer evening.

This really was a seductive experience, she thought. To be complimented, enticed by a man she didn't know, and who didn't know her, and whose attention seemed to be fixed intensely on her. No wonder the Venetian Festival was so popular!

She moistened her lips with the tip of her tongue, that butterfly fluttering in her stomach increasing as she sensed his dark gaze watching the movement.

'Come, Bella, what is your fantasy? Tonight I will be whoever you wish me to be.'

Dani hadn't even known she had a fantasy until now. 'Morgan,' she breathed. 'I would like to call you Morgan.'

'After the pirate Henry Morgan?' the pirate said with a nod. 'It is appropriate.'

Dani tilted her head. 'Although I somehow think you must be a relative of Eleni's…?'

He laughed. 'No names. No personal details. Those are the rules, are they not? Now, would you care to dance? Or perhaps a walk in the garden would be more to your liking?'

Dani eyed the dozen or so couples moving slowly to the music on the temporary dance floor that had been set up in front of the small orchestra, tempted by the idea of being taken in his arms—more than tempted. But did she really want to be that close to a man who already made her feel like behaving more recklessly than she ever had before?

For the moment, no…

'A walk, I think,' she accepted, careful not to touch him this time as he took the champagne glass from her and placed both of them on the tray of a passing waiter.

Despite her care in not touching him, he immediately took hold of her hand and placed it in the crook of his arm as they strolled through the dimly lit garden. His arm felt like tempered steel beneath her fingertips, the billowy sleeves of his shirt hardly any barrier to the heat of his skin at all.

Niccolo, sensing that his Belladonna was about to remove her hand from his arm, moved to place his other hand over the top of hers, determined not to relinquish this small contact with her.

She was enchanting, tiny perfection, her hand small and delicate beneath his much larger one, and the coloured lanterns and the light of the moon threw the beauty of her breasts and the bareness of her arms into shadowed relief.

He could never remember being this immediately attracted to any woman before. The muted lighting and softly romantic music no doubt added to the seduction of the evening, but nevertheless Niccolo knew it was the intriguing air of mystery that surrounded the woman at his side that gave such enchantment to the meeting and held him captive.

For once he didn't have to be the respected and respectable Niccolo D'Alessandro. His anonymity allowed him to be bolder, less reserved than was his normal custom. And he already knew where he wanted that boldness to take him with this woman… No doubt Eleni would be able to tell him exactly who his Belladonna was if he were to ask her, but Niccolo found that he didn't want to do that, preferring to savour each new discovery about this woman as it emerged.

He turned to her in concern as he felt the slight tremor of her tiny fingers beneath his. 'Are you cold?' he enquired as he looked down at her.

Those softly pouting lips curved into an enigmatic smile. 'Not at all,' she assured him.

Cold? Dani's thoughts echoed shakily. She was so

aware of this man, so sensitised to the almost feline strength of his body as he walked beside her, to the touch of the fingers that curved so possessively about hers, that she wasn't sure she could even think straight, let alone know whether she was hot or cold!

She was hot, she discovered when she concentrated on the question. Hot, hot, *hot*!

Every part of her felt tinglingly alive, and she was totally aware of the man beside her as she breathed shallowly, her breasts feeling full, her nipples hard and oh so sensitive as they pressed against her corset.

Again Niccolo felt the slight quiver of this woman's fingers beneath his. 'You *are* cold,' he insisted.

'Well—perhaps a little,' she allowed breathlessly.

Niccolo's gaze was riveted on the fullness of her slightly parted lips as she looked up at him. Their softness was an invitation he was finding it more and more difficult to resist.

He could no longer resist!

She tasted of champagne and honey, those lips as soft and delicious as Niccolo had imagined they would be. He gathered her close against him and feasted, sipping, tasting, deepening the kiss as he felt the surge of desire course through his body when he moulded her slender curves against him.

Dani was lost from the first moment those firmly sculptured lips claimed hers. And as she felt the leashed power behind her pirate's kiss, the hard throb of his thighs against hers, she knew that he wanted to do much more than just kiss her.

And, dear Lord, she wanted so much more than that too!

Tonight she wanted to forget everything else but this man and the seduction of the evening. Wanted to lose herself in the passion of his kisses and the promised pleasure of the hardness of his body.

She wanted him. Wildly. Frantically. Heatedly.

The realisation shocked her at the same time as she pressed her body longingly against his, her arms moving up about the broadness of his shoulders as her lips parted to deepen the kiss.

Nothing else mattered other than the intensity of the desire, the arousal, that surged through her body. The need to feel. To live only for this moment and to hell with tomorrow.

She moaned low in her throat as his hand moved from her waist to her breast, lingering there, cupping her, those long, warm fingers a caress on the bareness of her skin above the gown before they dipped lower, seeking and finding the hardened nub, and that single touch across the sensitised tip sent rivulets of pleasure throbbing between her thighs.

Her pirate's hands moved to cup her bottom and pull her against his thighs, against the rigid hardness there that told her of his own arousal. At the same time his tongue moved erotically across her bottom lip before surging beyond, capturing, claiming, as he tasted every part of her.

Niccolo wanted this woman now.

Right now!

His earlier aversion to couples disappearing off into the trees was totally forgotten as he held the woman of his dreams in his arms and tasted and caressed her with the same burning need, only the two of them existing as their kisses deepened hungrily.

Then a teasing laugh from somewhere amongst the shelter of the trees permeated the desire that had clouded his brain, and he drew abruptly back to rest his forehead against hers, his breathing ragged.

'I think perhaps we should go somewhere a little more—private. Do you agree?' he murmured ruefully.

She hesitated only fractionally before giving an affirmative nod of her head.

Niccolo moved back slightly, his hand sliding caressingly down her arm before he laced his fingers with her much smaller ones, only lingering long enough to once more kiss her hungrily on the lips before he turned to guide her towards the relative privacy of his sister's home.

Dani felt slightly dazed by the intensity of her arousal, was beyond thought, beyond anything but being the focus of this man's single-minded desire.

She wanted to be naked with him, wanted to touch and caress the broadness of his muscled back, ached to feel all that nakedness against her own. There would be plenty of time tomorrow, all her tomorrows, to be the much more cautious and emotionally bruised Dani Bell.

On paper she was a twenty-four-year-old divorcee. But the reality was different—so totally different.

Her disaster of a marriage to Philip had made her wary of men and physical relationships. As Eleni had once pointed out so succinctly, there had been no one in her life since the end of her marriage to Philip two and a half years ago.

The failure of that marriage had made her doubt her own attractiveness to men. But there was no doubting that her pirate found her attractive, that he wanted her, and part of her so ached to feel wanted, to feel desired, if not loved.

Nevertheless, she kept a wary eye out for Eleni as she and her pirate strolled back towards the house; she would never hear the end of it if her friend should spot Dani disappearing with one of her D'Alessandro cousins!

'I do not intend to do anything you do not want me to do,' Niccolo promised as he sensed the onset of doubt in the woman who walked so gracefully and silently beside him. At least he *hoped* he would have the control not to take things any further than this woman wanted them to go.

The reality was he wanted her so badly that his normally rigid control was in jeopardy of deserting him. Only the earlier interruption of that laugh had stopped him from enticing her into the trees with him and making love to her right then and there.

This immediacy was totally out of character for Niccolo.

There had been many women in his life over the last twenty years, and some of them had become a mistress for several months, but with none of them had he felt this driving need to know, to touch, to make love until they were both weak and satiated. And then start all over again.

Eleni's conservatory was in darkness as Niccolo opened the door and allowed the woman at his side to enter first, before closing and locking the door firmly behind them, shutting out the noise of the other partygoers and all but the muted strains of the small orchestra.

Dani's hand moved to cover his as he would have switched on one of the lamps. 'It's more—in keeping with the evening this way,' she whispered, inwardly knowing that if he switched on a light the magic of this encounter would be broken and she would run away—probably screaming.

Philip's uncontrollable and unwarranted jealousy had made Dani not just wary, but actually fearful of physical relationships, and she was sure that the only thing that was giving her courage now was the mask each of them was wearing and the anonymity the darkness afforded.

In fact, the veritable forest of exotic plants and trees that Eleni nurtured in her conservatory effected such a feeling of privacy, of heightened expectancy, that it seemed to Dani as if the two of them were alone on some lush desert island. Which was very fitting, considering he was dressed as a pirate!

'You've been here before?' he asked, as Dani confidently made her way to where the sofa and chairs were situated.

'Once or twice,' she replied, not wanting to give away even that much of herself.

Behaving with uncharacteristic recklessness was one thing, having this man discover her identity as Eleni's best friend was something else entirely!

She turned to face him, stepping closer to let her hands slide slowly up his silk-covered chest. 'We aren't supposed to be asking personal questions, remember?'

'I remember,' he murmured, as his arms moved about her waist to draw her close against him and his head lowered so that his lips could claim hers.

Heaven.

There was absolutely no other way for Dani to describe the pleasure that surged through her as the kiss deepened, as her lips parted to the silky caress of his tongue before it slowly entered her mouth.

Oh, God!

Dani's legs went weak at this slow, sensuous plundering, her arms tightening on his shoulders as she clung. He moulded her against him from breast to thigh, their legs entwined.

It had been too long, she acknowledged achingly. Far too long. And it had never been like this before. Ever.

Dani's head swam, her body feeling completely, totally alive as the man she knew only as Morgan continued to kiss her. His hands moved restlessly across her back before cupping her bottom and pulling her even tighter against him, allowing her once again to feel the heat of his arousal as her own thighs melted into liquid fire.

That heat intensified, became almost unbearable, as one of his hands caressed the bare tops of her breasts, igniting her so that she longed to have him caress her more fully, and her nipples were hard and aching for his touch as she pressed closer in silent appeal.

But the magic stopped, abruptly ceased, the moment she felt his hand move up to the ties at the back of her mask.

'No!' She broke the kiss to protest, breathing hard as she backed away slightly, cheeks burning, eyes feverish. 'No,' she repeated more calmly, as she sensed him looking at her questioningly. 'It's more—exciting this way, don't you think?'

More exciting? Niccolo mused wryly. If things became any more exciting the two of them were going to go up in flames! But perhaps she was right—perhaps it was the fact that they were both masked, their identities secret, that made this whole experience so uniquely erotic.

She moved her body enticingly against his, the elusive perfume of her skin, the way her breasts swelled above her low-cut gown, once again holding him in thrall.

Niccolo drew in a sharp breath as his body pulsed,

throbbed in answer to all that she was offering. 'I—' He broke off as she pressed her fingertips against his mouth and played them lightly over his bottom lip before one dipped provocatively inside in silent invitation.

An invitation Niccolo was powerless to resist.

He held her against him and his tongue moved moistly across her finger, licking, enticing, making it hot and wet. The same way Niccolo wanted *her* as she lay beneath him. Or on top of him. He didn't care which…

CHAPTER TWO

DANI quivered with excitement, with anticipation, as she turned in silent invitation and allowed him to slide the zip of her gown down the length of her spine, groaning low in her throat as his lips followed the same path before he straightened once again to turn her to face him.

She breathed shallowly as she lowered her arms to allow the gown to fall shimmering to the floor. She slipped her feet out of the gold slippers and dispensed with the cumbersome hoops to stand before him wearing only the tight corset with matching cream silk French knickers.

'No, leave it,' he growled throatily as Dani would have reached up to undo the twenty or so hooks down the front of the corset. His gaze was intent on her masked face as he threw off his waistcoat and the black sash before moving to stand in front of her. 'I have always wondered what it would be like to remove one of these,' he admitted. 'I am going to very much enjoy finding out.' His accent had thickened in his deepening desire.

Dani hoped that it felt as sensually arousing to him as it did to her as he slowly undid the hooks, one by one, as he savoured the moment her breasts were free and he could brush his fingers lightly over their pouting tips. Dani's breath caught in her throat as he lightly caressed the taut and swollen nipples.

She felt her knees go weak as he lowered his head and his lips claimed one temptingly pert bud, his tongue licking slowly, rhythmically, making her skin wet. Her nipple swelled in arousal inside his mouth as his teeth gently rasped against that sensitivity and he continued to taste and suckle.

Her hands moved up instinctively to cradle the back of his head and she held him to her, her back arched, her breathing ragged as pleasure surged hotly between her thighs and dampened her until she was hot and aching.

He moved the attentions of his lips and tongue to her other breast, licking, gently biting, while his hand captured its twin and caressed that hardened nub in the same pleasurable rhythm.

God, she was so excited, so aroused, Dani realised in trembling wonder. She was going to explode into a million pieces right here and now while this man was still fully dressed and she was wearing only her panties!

Her fingers clenched in the dark thickness of his hair as she held him against her. He increased the rhythm of his caressing tongue and his other hand moved from her breast to seek lower, cupping between her thighs. The pad of his palm pressed subtly, rhythmically, against the hardened nub nestling there. Pressing, caressing, until Dani felt an aching pleasure all centred there, before it spread out to every part of her body, hot and fierce, totally encompassing, and she arched against his caressing hand in a climax that seemed never ending.

Her knees buckled slightly and her head dropped forward to rest against the broadness of his shoulder as those spasms of pleasure finally began to lessen, her breathing ragged and sporadic.

'I don't— I've never— That was so—'

'You are beautiful!' Niccolo assured her with husky force even as his arms moved about her and he lifted her up to carry her to the sofa. He laid her down on its length, his gaze once again holding hers captive as he straightened to begin unbuttoning his shirt.

No woman had ever looked more beautiful to him, the glow of the moonlight giving her skin the appearance of alabaster against the cream silk underwear she wore, her eyes dark and satiated behind her mask. The posture of her body—turned slightly sideways on the sofa, with those small graceful hands resting on her thighs and the long silken legs bent slightly at the knees—was sensually enticing.

Niccolo left his shirt unbuttoned, revealing the dark hair of his chest and the flatness of his stomach, as his fingers dealt deftly with the fastening of his trousers.

'Let me.' She held her hand out in invitation. 'It's my turn to undress you,' she whispered, moving over on the sofa to make room for him to lie down beside her.

No part of Niccolo found objection to that invitation— not the surge in his already hardened shaft, the increased beat of his heart, or the clamouring inside him to feel those delicate hands against his naked body.

And God, those hands felt good as she pushed the sides of his shirt aside to lay them flat against his chest, light as butterfly wings as she moved up beside him, expression sultry, her bottom lip caught between tiny, even white teeth as she looked her fill of him and her hands touched and caressed him from shoulder to thigh.

Niccolo breathed in sharply, his stomach tightening, as one hand moved lower, beneath the waistband of his trousers, and she touched him lightly before curling her fingers about his rigid hardness.

He felt like steel encased in silk, Dani discovered as she pushed aside his clothing to slowly caress his arousal from tip to base and then back again. She revelled in the response of his long thickness as he moved slowly, sensuously, against her hand and fingers, in the increased raggedness of his breathing as her thumb caressed the sensitive tip and she felt the slight escape of moisture.

But she wanted more. Wanted it all. To taste him, not just touch and caress him.

She moved up on her knees beside him to slide his trousers and boxers down the long length of his legs and drop them down on the carpet beside them, holding his gaze as she parted his legs to move in between them and cup and hold him.

Then she finally looked down at him. He was long, hard and beautiful, she acknowledged, even as she lowered her head to capture him in her mouth, feeling emboldened, empowered, as she heard his groan of acceptance and surrender.

His hands came up to grasp her shoulders—not to push her away, as she had initially disappointedly thought, but to plead with her not to stop that rasping caress of her tongue or the rhythmic caress of her hands as she cupped and held him.

His groans became deeper, more ragged, with each

caress, and Dani wallowed in his pleasure as surely as if it were her own.

It *was* her own!

She had never known anything like this before, had never felt so uninhibited, so free to express her enjoyment in a man's body. In *this* man's body.

It was a beautiful, perfect male body, muscled and yet silky, his shoulders wide, his stomach flat, his thighs—Oh, God, his thighs…

'No more, little one!' he suddenly rasped fiercely, his fingers tight on her shoulders as he sat up to gently hold her away from him. 'I want to take off the rest of your clothes. Slowly. And then I want to kiss and caress you in the way you have just kissed me,' he explained.

Dani smiled as she knelt back to lift her own breasts to his dark, appreciative gaze before he lowered his head to draw one of those darkened nipples into his mouth as he slid the silk panties down her thighs.

In seconds she knelt completely, unashamedly naked in front of him, knowing by the raggedness of his breathing and the intensity of that dark gaze that he liked what he saw.

It was exhilarating, liberating, to be with a man like this, to just enjoy without doubt or responsibility…

She was perfection in the moonlight, Niccolo acknowledged achingly as she slid the shirt from his shoulders and down his arms. Her breasts full and pert, her waist slender, hips curvaceous, a lush triangle of hair at their apex, and her smile enticing as she lay back against the cushions.

He reached up and removed his mask—it had to be past midnight now—before bending to kiss first one dark-tipped breast and then the other, his hands dark against her much paler flesh as he trailed yet more kisses down her stomach to her navel, dipping his tongue into that sensitive well as he moved to lie between her parted legs.

Her skin was like velvet, and she groaned her pleasure at each stroke of his hand, that groan becoming a soft mewling noise as he moved lower still, seeking and finding the hardened nub between those silken curls to roll his tongue against it slowly, rhythmically, caressingly.

Dani felt boneless as waves of pleasure washed up and through her, turning to rigid tension as she felt another climax rapidly approaching.

It was too much—

She couldn't—

'Please,' she whispered. 'I want— I need—'

'Tell me what you need and want, my beautiful lady,' he encouraged gruffly.

'You,' she gasped, reaching down for him, fingernails digging into those broad shoulders. 'I need you!'

'Then you shall have me,' Niccolo assured her, moving up and over her. 'All of me.'

He gave a primeval groan as he entered her and buried himself inside her heat. He didn't move again for long, pleasurable seconds, just enjoying being inside her, and then he raised his head to watch the play of moonlight across her firm breasts with their deep rose tips.

Perhaps it really was the mystery that surrounded this woman, but he had never felt such incredible excitement, such intense pleasure, as he did here and now. Then he began to move slowly, and he knew that the pleasure that had come before was as nothing compared to what he was feeling now.

The pleasure intensified, grew hotter, stronger, until Niccolo wasn't sure he could bear more without exploding. He began to stroke deep inside her, his body gliding over and in hers as she began to make soft noises of excitement.

Niccolo held off as long as he could, promising himself to take longer next time, to take her to the edge of that peak again and again before taking her over it. But for now the need for release was too urgent, too intense for him to delay. And as he heard the first of her cries of release, felt her tighten and flex hotly about him, he allowed himself to let go too. A release made all the stronger, all the more satisfying, because they had reached it together.

Dani lay entwined with her pirate, their bodies slicked with sweat in the aftermath of their lovemaking. She stroked the loosened, overlong darkness of his hair as his head rested between her breasts. Both of them were too satiated to even attempt to move, and still too afraid of breaking the spell, the magic of the evening, by so much as saying one word.

And it had been magical. Beyond anything Dani had ever experienced before. This man had allowed her the freedom to explore and caress his body in a way she had never dared to do before with anyone else.

This man made her feel beautiful. She was beautiful in his arms. And that he had enjoyed their lovemaking too she was in absolutely no doubt. She could feel his satisfaction in the way he still caressed her body from breast to thigh— not in a sexual way, but out of the sheer pleasure of touching her.

But as she lay there in the silence, as she slowly became

aware of their surroundings, could once again hear the muted strains of the music and the people laughing and talking outside, the full import of what had just happened hit her like a slap in the face.

Dear God—there was recklessness and then there was *insanity*! And this, Dani realised belatedly, was insanity. She had made love with a perfect stranger—probably one of Eleni's *relatives*—in her friend's conservatory. And she continued to lie here naked in his arms when there were over two hundred guests outside in the garden!

Beautiful, ecstatic insanity. But insanity nonetheless.

And now it was over.

It had to be over...

'Have you fallen asleep?' Niccolo asked teasingly at the sudden stillness and silence of the woman who had such a short time ago met and equalled his desire in the most incredible, most erotic lovemaking he had ever known.

Their clothes, he noticed ruefully, were scattered all over the rug beside the sofa, their need for skin on skin having been absolute. He wanted this woman like that again. And again. Not here, in his sister's home, where they could be interrupted at any moment, but somewhere they could be completely themselves, where there would be no need for masks or artifice.

He wanted to know more about this woman—wanted to know everything there was to know about her. Wanted to look at her face, to see her wearing her long hair loose about her shoulders and nothing else.

'Would you like to leave?' he murmured. 'We could book into a hotel somewhere. For a week. A month. Longer!'

At this moment the world of D'Alessandro Banking seemed unimportant. She was the only thing that mattered right now—and for some time to come, he felt sure.

'Belladonna…?' he prompted as he raised his head to look down at her.

Dani gave a muted gasp, and then ceased to breathe at all as she recognised the unmasked beauty of the face above hers in the moonlight.

Her heart seemed to stop beating and the blood froze in her veins.

The world itself seemed to stop spinning on its axis.

The man above her, lying naked beside her, the man she had just made love with so wonderfully, so completely, was *Niccolo D'Alessandro*!

'What is it, *cara mia*?' He frowned down at her with concern. 'Do not tell me that you are suddenly feeling shy?' he teased.

Shy? After the intimacies she had just shared with this man?

Niccolo D'Alessandro…

And she had—

And then he had—

Oh, Lord.

But Niccolo obviously had no more idea of her true identity than she'd had of his. There was no way he would have flirted with Dani Bell in that way. Would have seduced Dani Bell so single-mindedly in the moonlight. Would have made love to Dani Bell with such intensity and passion.

He *couldn't* know it was her!

The D'Alessandro ancestors had been priests, princes— and *pirates*, she belatedly recalled.

And she couldn't bear for this pirate to realise who his lover was. To have the warmth fade from those beautiful dark eyes as they assumed their usual expression of contempt whenever he looked at her. But how could she get out of here without Niccolo discovering the truth?

He had given her the opening himself, she realised with dawning hope.

She moistened her lips before speaking. 'A hotel sounds good. But I don't think we should leave without at least one of us making our excuses to Eleni or Brad.'

Dani's thoughts were racing now. If Niccolo left the conservatory to talk to Eleni or Brad, and if she could get dressed quickly enough, she might—just might—be able to get out of here and away from the house before Niccolo came back.

'The two of us going to a hotel together only sounds "good"?' His expression was amused as he moved to sit beside her on the sofa before turning to trail light fingertips over her body from her throat down to her thighs.

Dani trembled as her body instantly came alive to his touch, her nipples hardening, tightening to aroused pebbles, and the heat returning between her thighs.

This was *Niccolo*, she reminded herself impatiently. The man who made no secret of his utter contempt for her.

'More than good. Wonderful,' she corrected abruptly, just wanting him to leave so that she could get out of here.

'That is better.' Niccolo nodded his satisfaction, his gaze hooded as he stood up. 'I will not be long,' he promised as he moved to pull on his clothes, steeling himself not to lie back down beside her and make love to her all over again.

But there would be plenty of time for that once they

reached the hotel. Plenty of time to learn all there was to know about this beautiful and responsive woman.

Niccolo could never remember feeling such possessiveness before during a relationship—this need to know a woman in every way. Perhaps that was because this wasn't a relationship. Yet. But it was going to be. He didn't intend letting this woman out of his life, his bed, until they had completely slaked their desire for each other.

Which could take some time, he decided, when he only had to look at her for his body to harden with renewed desire!

'The sooner you leave…' Dani encouraged, with a lightness she was far from feeling.

The realisation that she had just made love with Niccolo still made her feel weak at the knees, and she was only just managing to hold down her nausea as she imagined the darkness of his rage if he should learn her identity tonight.

But there was no reason why he should ever find out who she was—if Dani could just manage to get away before he returned…

'Five minutes,' he stated as he strode forcefully towards the door.

Dani's encouraging smile vanished as soon as Niccolo had gone.

She had only minutes in which to dress and leave—to escape like one pursued!

It couldn't be done!

It *had* to be done, Dani decided grimly as she quickly began to throw her clothes back on. Not the corset. She really didn't have time for all those hooks just now—

If she could just make it to the front door undetected she

could make good her escape—would walk all the way back home if she had to.

Once there she didn't ever have to open her door again. Never had to see Niccolo D'Alessandro ever again…

CHAPTER THREE

'DANI! I've been trying to contact you all day; where on earth are you?' Eleni demanded late on Sunday evening, when Dani finally took the call on her mobile.

Dani was well aware of the fact that Eleni had been trying to reach her all day—she had just chosen not answer any of her friend's telephone calls until now.

Mainly because she had no idea what to say to her. Or what Eleni was going to say. Surely that all depended on whether or not Eleni was aware of Dani's...*encounter* with her brother the previous evening?

'I'm at Wiverley Hall.'

'What are you doing there?' Eleni sounded puzzled.

Good question!

Hiding, seemed to pretty well answer it...

Dani had come up with the idea of visiting her parents—of removing herself from London completely—as she'd tried to find a taxi after the masquerade to take her back into the city. She had realised that to stay at her apartment was unthinkable. Niccolo could come storming over at any moment demanding an explanation for her behaviour, once he discovered she had been the woman in the gold gown.

Because it was inevitable that he would find out eventually. After all, Eleni knew exactly which of her female guests had been dressed in the gold gown and mask the previous evening, and Niccolo only had to ask her to find out the unwelcome truth.

Of course there was always the possibility that Niccolo, having returned to the conservatory to find his mystery lady had flown, would be too angry or too proud to actually ask his sister who the woman in the gold gown had been. But as Dani recalled the intensity of the passion they had shared, along with Niccolo's determination to spend the rest of the night with her, she knew it was very likely a remote hope.

'Visiting my parents and grandfather, of course,' she said with false lightness.

'You left last night without saying goodbye,' Eleni reproved.

'I did try, but I couldn't find you in all the crush.'

'Dani?'

'Yes?'

Eleni's sigh could be heard. 'Dani, Niccolo looked for you last night after you left without saying goodbye.'

'For me?' She feigned surprise even as her fingers tightened about her mobile. 'Why on earth would he do that?'

'Dani, please don't,' her friend rebuked her gently. 'I *know* you were the woman with Niccolo last night, and that's why you left the party so suddenly.'

Dani sat down abruptly on the bed in the bedroom that had been hers since childhood. But she didn't see the rosettes she had won as a child at gymkhanas still pinned on the wall. Or the long shelves of books. Or the pretty lace canopy over the bed that had been added when she was a teenager. All Dani could see was Niccolo D'Alessandro's face. His incredibly angry face…

'Does Niccolo know the woman was me?' she breathed tremulously, abandoning all hope of convincing Eleni that she had no idea what she was talking about.

'Not yet,' Eleni said. 'But he's going to,' she warned. 'I feigned complete ignorance last night when he sought me out and pressed me to tell him who the woman in the gold gown had been, but I doubt I'll be able to keep the truth from him for long. Dani, what did you and Niccolo *do* last night?'

What *hadn't* they done? That was probably more the question!

Just thinking about the previous evening, the intimacies she had shared with Niccolo, was enough to make Dani blush—unbecomingly—to the roots of her red hair.

She rushed into speech. 'I didn't know it was him, okay? You've always made such a big thing about your Venetian cousins, how handsome and charming they all are—that I just assumed it was one of them when he began to flirt with me.'

'Niccolo *flirted* with you?' Eleni sounded disbelieving.

He had done a lot more than flirt. They both had.

Dani had never behaved like that in her life before.

And she would never behave like that again either!

Not now she recognised there was no such thing as pleasure without responsibility.

'Yes,' she confirmed huskily. 'I—I didn't know it was Niccolo!'

'You already said that,' Eleni pointed out dryly. 'Didn't you pick up on my hint about the D'Alessandro ancestry?'

'If I had, do you really think I would have spent the evening with your arrogant brother?' she groaned.

'Probably not,' Eleni allowed.

'Eleni, you *can't* think that I wanted to— That I ever intended to spend the evening with Niccolo, of all people?' she gasped incredulously.

'I really don't know what to think, Dani,' her friend replied. 'All I know is that my big brother is behaving completely out of character and insisting on finding the mystery woman he met last night at my masquerade party.'

Niccolo was still looking for her? Dani gulped.

No, he wasn't looking for her, she reassured herself. Niccolo was looking for the woman who had attracted him the previous evening.

The woman who had returned that attraction.

The woman who'd had wild sex with him in his sister's conservatory!

Dani had never experienced anything like it in her life before, and she still felt hot all over just at the thought of it.

'You were the one who told me that was what the masks were for,' she reminded her friend defensively. 'So that people could behave out of character safely hidden behind them.'

'How "out of character" did you behave, Dani?' Eleni asked.

'Very,' she answered tightly.

'How very…?'

'Very, *very*.'

'Oh.'

'Eleni, are you going to tell Niccolo it was me?'

'It isn't a question of my telling or not telling, Dani. Brad knows it was you, too,' Eleni warned. 'So far Niccolo hasn't thought to ask him about the woman in the gold gown, but it's probably only a matter of time...'

'He'll forget about me in a few days, and then—'

'Niccolo doesn't forget *anything*,' Eleni interrupted ruthlessly. 'And whatever the two of you did last night it certainly seems to have made an impact.'

'Eleni, *please*—'

'Dani, tell me that none of this has anything to do with your grandfather's will.'

'My grandfa—?' Dani was stunned. 'What on earth do you mean, Eleni?'

'If you remember, I once joked about you seducing one of my cousins...'

'Eleni, you can't *seriously* think that I— You don't think that I would *deliberately*—' Dani was beyond stunned now—she was speechless.

'Actually, Dani, I don't believe what *I* think is all that important, do you?'

Dani became very still as the full import of the possible consequences of last night struck her.

Eight months ago her grandfather had changed his will to stipulate that Dani had to provide a Bell heir before he died, or her parents would lose their home as well as their living.

And last night Dani had made love with a man she had believed to be a complete stranger, which was completely out of character for her.

All of which Eleni knew.

She had obviously drawn her own conclusions about Dani's motives for her uncharacteristic behaviour the previous evening. Conclusions that Niccolo, if he learnt of that clause in her grandfather's will, would no doubt also draw.

Eleni was right. It didn't matter what she personally thought of Dani's behaviour the previous evening; it was what Niccolo believed that was going to be important…

'Your mother told me I would find you out here.'

Dani almost fell over the bucket of feed she had given her horse while she rubbed him down after her morning ride as she heard the grimness of Niccolo D'Alessandro's voice just behind her.

Niccolo was here—at her parents' home in Gloucestershire?

Dani's movements were measured, carefully precise, as she placed the brush down on the straw before straightening to rub her wet hands nervously down the thighs of her jeans and then slowly turn to face Niccolo. A Niccolo who looked as grim-faced as his tone had implied he was going to be.

There was no mistaking the tension of his body either. In a black tee shirt that stretched tautly over those wide shoulders and fitted jeans, it was as if he were barely repressing his anger.

As if?

If Niccolo was here for the reason Dani thought he was, then there was no doubting he was angry. No—furious, she amended as she found herself unable to break her own gaze away from the intensity of his glacial brown eyes.

'Niccolo.' She forced the muscles in her face to relax as she moved to look at him enquiringly over Jet's back. 'What on earth are you doing here?'

'Do I *really* need to spell it out, Daniella?' Those dark eyes glittered dangerously.

She would rather that he didn't. She had spent the last few days convincing herself that her time in his arms hadn't happened at all! But with Niccolo standing only feet away, and with every nerve ending in her body, every one of her senses, screaming her awareness of him, that was no longer an option.

She knew this man. Had touched and caressed every part of him. And no amount of wishing otherwise was ever going to change that.

Perhaps that saying should be Act in haste, repent at leisure? From the anger she could feel emanating in her direction from Niccolo's rigid body he was going to do more than make her repent.

'The two of us need to go somewhere and talk,' he said icily when she didn't answer him, and that coldness sent a chill of apprehension down Dani's spine.

She wasn't ready for this—would she ever be? She had simply naively hoped as the days, almost a week, had crawled past, with no sign of Niccolo, that he must have returned to Venice without finding out the identity of his mystery woman.

One glance at Niccolo's absolutely livid expression and Dani knew that was no longer true...

'Talk about what, Niccolo?' she stalled lightly, at the same time continuing to keep the black stallion that her father had given her for her twenty-first birthday between them. Jet shifted restlessly in his stall as he obviously sensed her tension.

Niccolo's mouth twisted scathingly. 'Oh, I think you

know, Daniella. Or should I call you *Belladonna*?' he added, his voice now lethally soft.

Dani's stomach felt as if the bottom had just dropped out of it, and she could feel her hands begin to tremble as she fought for breath.

This confrontation was worse, so much worse than she had ever imagined that it would be. In those imaginings she had been able to laugh off the incident as unimportant, as just a bit of fun. Niccolo didn't look as if he found any of this in the least amusing. Or ever would!

But she tried again. 'Belladonna?' She shook her head. 'I have no idea what you're talking about—'

'Do not even *try* to deny it was you that night, Daniella!' Niccolo cut in harshly, not in any sort of mood to play games.

He had spent all his time these last few days discreetly eliminating every woman who had been at Eleni and Brad's party that evening, finally coming down to the one woman no one could account for.

Daniella Bell.

Incredible as that possibility had seemed to him at first, the more Niccolo had thought about it the more it had become a reality. The woman in gold had been the right height and size to be Daniella, and the white powder would have hidden the brightness of her red hair. And she would easily have been able to disguise the normally brisk tone with which she normally addressed him with that huskily seductive, totally unrecognisable voice.

It had been a little more difficult imagining that Daniella could possibly be the sexily uninhibited woman who had made love with him. But having openly confronted Eleni this morning, Niccolo now knew that woman had indeed been Daniella Bell.

Incredible, but nevertheless true.

And his anger hadn't abated in the least during his drive to Gloucestershire in order that he might confront Daniella with the truth face to face. In fact it had settled like a cold, leaden weight in his chest.

Daniella's evasiveness now, as she shot him apprehensive glances from beneath lowered dark lashes, only increased the intensity of that fury.

She was wise to feel apprehensive—at the moment Niccolo was clenching his hands into fists at his sides in an effort to stop himself from reaching out and wringing her slender neck!

'Why did you do it, Daniella?' he growled.

'Why?' she echoed hollowly.

He nodded grimly. 'Explain to me why you made love with me that night and then disappeared before I could discover who you really were.'

Dani drew in a ragged breath. 'Niccolo—'

'Could we get out of here?' he asked impatiently as Jet swung his head dangerously close to him and bared his teeth. 'Your horse obviously does not like me,' he added dryly.

She moved to run a soothing hand down the length of Jet's nose. 'You're making him nervous.'

'And you?' Niccolo spoke softly—dangerously so. 'Am I making you nervous too, Daniella?'

He was frightening the life out of her, if the truth were known!

Niccolo cutting and sarcastic she was used to. Niccolo

totally indifferent to her she could accept too. But this Niccolo, cold and threatening, his anger barely leashed, was terrifying.

But damn it, he had been a willing participant that night—more than willing! And he couldn't deny that he had enjoyed it because he had been the one to suggest they book into a hotel so that they might continue doing more of the same.

Her chin rose as her gaze met his challengingly. 'Why are you making such a fuss, Niccolo?' she asked waspishly. 'We're both over the age of consent, and you can't deny we had a good time that night.' She shrugged slender shoulders. 'So why can't you just leave it at that, hmm?'

Because he couldn't do it. That was why. Much as he had tried, Niccolo hadn't been able to get the memory of the woman in the gold gown out of his head—hadn't been able to forget making love with her.

He had been so determined to find her again that he had delayed his return to Venice by several days in order to continue his search.

He still found it incredible that his search had ultimately led him to this woman.

Had she known it was him that night?

Had she known and found all the more pleasure— amusement, perhaps?—in knowing that Niccolo had no idea with whom he was making love?

He had questions, many of them, and he did not intend leaving until Daniella had answered them all.

His impatience was not improved by the fact that at this moment he was completely aware of Daniella, in the over-large tee shirt she was wearing over fitted jodhpurs and brown riding boots. That he knew exactly what she looked like beneath those clothes and how to caress and kiss that body in order to give her the ultimate in pleasure.

His mouth tightened. 'I have no intention of *just leaving* anything, Daniella,' he rasped. 'I want an explanation for your behaviour last weekend, and I want it *now*!'

She shook her head. 'I'm busy, Niccolo—'

'You will get yourself out of that stall right now, Daniella, or I will come in and get you!' he threatened.

He would too, Dani acknowledged heavily. Even Jet's restless movements, the stamping of his hooves, wouldn't deter Niccolo if he decided to come in and get her.

'Fine—I'll walk you back to your car,' she snapped, giving Jet one last reassuring pat before moving to the stall door. 'But I really don't have anything else to say about last Saturday,' she told him as she let herself out into the yard.

It was busy at this time of the day, all the stable lads and girls having returned from their early-morning canter and now rubbing down and feeding their mounts. Their chatter and laughter was at complete odds with the feeling of rapidly increasing doom that held Dani in its grip.

'Eleni told me these are your father's stables,' Niccolo remarked evenly as the two of them left the busy yard and walked in the direction of the huge manor house.

Dani eyed him warily. 'Yes.'

'I believe he is very well thought of as a trainer?'

'Yes.'

'I suppose you have been riding since before you could walk?'

'More or less.'

'Daniella, can you not at least give me credit for trying to effect some semblance of normality by conversing in this way?' Niccolo glared down the length of his arrogant nose at her.

Normality? How could anything possibly be *normal* between the two of them ever again?

Maybe she should have thought of that last weekend?

Maybe she would have done if she had realised her pirate Morgan was actually Niccolo D'Alessandro!

But she couldn't really say she had been thinking at all that night. She had simply savoured the moment and allowed herself to forget all her troubles, if only for a short time. She had been as devastated that night at discovering Niccolo was her pirate as he probably was now at finding out she was his Belladonna.

She couldn't even look at Niccolo now without remembering the intimacies they had shared—the response of his body to her caresses, the pleasure she had felt as he thrust deep inside her…

This was *not* helping, Dani rebuked herself impatiently.

'Perhaps you would like me to comment on the weather?' she taunted him naughtily. 'I believe that's always good for a few minutes' normal conversation.'

Niccolo turned to give her a narrow-eyed glare, his mouth tightening even further as his frustrated anger deepened dangerously.

If Daniella imagined this was any more comfortable for him than it was for her, that driving to her parents' home in order to confront her with the truth had been easy for him to do, then she was mistaken. She was the last woman Niccolo would have chosen to have this conversation with!

Niccolo turned to look down at her as they reached the black sports car he kept garaged at his house in England. The warm breeze ruffled the fiery length of her hair, revealing the wide brow and high cheekbones that had been hidden by a mask the last time the two of them had talked. Talked? They hadn't really talked at all—they had been too busy kissing and pleasuring each other to talk!

He had to stop thinking about that night, Niccolo told himself sternly. Maybe it *had* been the most sexually enjoyable night of his life, but the reality—knowing it was Daniella Bell he had been making love with—surely made the whole thing ludicrous.

He did not even like her. He had not considered her a good influence on Eleni when the two girls were younger, even less so when Eleni came to London to go to university, and the fact that Daniella's brief marriage had barely survived the honeymoon had only served to confirm that she was no example for Eleni to emulate.

But somewhere in the last ten years, Niccolo acknowledged with grudging awareness, she had matured into a beautiful woman, her body slender and lithe, her movements graceful, her eyes a beautiful translucent green, her mouth—

No! He would not think about that perfect bow of a mouth, nor the way it had pleasured him almost a week ago!

'So?' She looked up at him challengingly. 'What is it you want to know, Niccolo?'

His mouth thinned at her aggression. 'I have already told you,' he bit out. 'I want to know why. I want to hear from your own lips exactly why you did what you did.'

Daniella raised auburn brows. 'Why I did what *I* did?' she retorted heatedly. 'I seem to recall that *you* were the one who talked to me first! Who asked me to walk with him? Who kissed *me*? Who suggested we go somewhere more private? I certainly don't remember hearing you complaining at the time!'

Of course Niccolo hadn't complained—he had been totally sexually enthralled!

As he knew he would be again if he should ever take this woman in his arms....

So long as the lights were out and he couldn't actually see who he was making love with!

'I am well aware of the sequence of events last Saturday evening, Daniella,' he snarled. 'And now I know exactly who they happened with!'

Her expression was scornful as she shook her head. 'If my identity is the only problem you have with what happened, then I suggest you just forget about it and move on.'

'Have *you* forgotten it, Daniella?'

Dani would never forget that night. Not one single moment of it.

It had been magical. Wonderful. Exhilarating. Liberating. And not even the fact that her lover had turned out to be Niccolo D'Alessandro could ever change that.

In fact, Dani had come to realise that knowing her lover was Niccolo only made it more memorable. The infatuation she'd felt for him ten years ago hadn't died or been crushed under the force of his cutting sarcasm, after all, but had deepened into something else. Something she had kept well hidden. Even from herself....

Maybe she hadn't consciously known it was Niccolo she was making love with on Saturday night, but had some inner part of her—some inner sense, the part of her that still found him so devastatingly attractive—actually told her who it was?

The more Dani thought about her impetuous behaviour that night, the more she believed it was more than a possibility.

But she had to protect herself. 'Of course I've forgotten all about it,' she lied.

Niccolo's eyes narrowed to dark slits as he spoke even more icily, if that were possible. 'So you make a habit of making love with men you do not even know and then conveniently forgetting about them?'

He'd meant to be insulting, Dani recognised heavily—and he had succeeded.

But if she defended herself, if she said no she didn't, then Niccolo was going to demand to know why she had made an exception in his case.

And her reasons were too complicated.

Or too simple!

There were those hidden feelings for him, of course, but there was also another explanation. She was tired, worn down by worry over her grandfather's will on her parents' behalf. The attention of her seductive pirate last weekend had lifted her out of all that, had transported her into another world—a world of light-hearted fun that had deepened into intense sexual tension and the indescribable pleasure that followed.

Not an excuse, perhaps, but it was certainly an explanation.

None of which she could possibly confide to Niccolo D'Alessandro!

'I don't make a habit of it, no,' she answered lightly. 'But I very much doubt I'm the first woman to indulge in a little—what was it you called it that night?—fantasy, I believe. *Morgan*,' she added pointedly, and was rewarded by a fierce frown. 'I certainly don't see why you're making such a big thing out of it.'

'You do not?' he grated.

'Not at all. After all—'

'You are the best friend of my sister,' Niccolo cut in furiously. 'Does that fact not make this a "big thing"?' he challenged.

Dani winced. It did make things a little awkward, she had to admit, and it was certainly not something that she and Eleni would ever be able to laugh about. But surely the awkwardness of the situation was for the two women to work out, not Niccolo?

'Hello, there!'

Dani flinched as she easily recognised her grandfather's strident tones, turning slowly to watch him as he strolled down the front steps of Wiverley Hall.

Still tall and erect, his bearing military even though he had retired from the army over twenty years ago, Daniel Bell had a full head of iron-grey hair and a neatly trimmed moustache. His clothes—a checked jacket over a twill shirt worn with brown corduroys—added to his 'country squire' image.

'We've been waiting for you to bring your visitor up to the house, Daniella,' he reproved as he joined them in the driveway.

Introducing Niccolo to any of her family—least of all

her tactlessly outspoken grandfather—was not something Dani wanted to do. But in the circumstances it seemed she had little choice…

'Grandfather, this is Niccolo D'Alessandro,' she said stiffly. 'Niccolo, my grandfather—Major Daniel Bell.'

'Sir.' Niccolo shook the other man's hand.

'D'Alessandro…' Her grandfather repeated slowly. 'Any connection with the D'Alessandro Bank?' He eyed the younger man speculatively.

Niccolo inclined his head. 'It is the family business, yes.'

Dani couldn't help but notice the increased speculation in her grandfather's shrewd expression. Obviously her grandfather was perfectly aware of the prestigious D'Alessandro Bank. And there was one thing that could be said about her grandfather—he was never averse to a little social snobbery!

'Well, I hope you've come here to cheer Daniella up, D'Alessandro,' her grandfather continued briskly. 'Girl's been moping around here for almost a week now—'

'Grandfather!' Dani exclaimed sharply, aware of the amused twist to Niccolo's mouth as he obviously enjoyed her discomfort.

Eyes the same colour green as her own met hers unapologetically. 'Only telling the truth, young lady. I trust my granddaughter has invited you to join us for lunch?' He turned his narrowed gaze on the younger man.

Dani's breath caught and held in her throat as she too turned to look at Niccolo.

She didn't want him to stay to lunch.

And she was pretty sure that Niccolo didn't want to accept the invitation, either.

But that didn't mean he wasn't going to…

CHAPTER FOUR

NICCOLO sensed Daniella's silent plea for him to refuse her grandfather's invitation to join her family for lunch. And a part of him—a large part, he had to admit— wanted to refuse. Now that he had confirmed it had been Daniella last weekend he just wanted to leave—to get as far away from her as he possibly could. But another part of him wanted something quite different....

'Niccolo has to get back to London. Don't you, Niccolo?' Daniella prompted, her gaze forceful as it met his.

He eyed her consideringly. That she wished him to leave— that she wished he had never come here in the first place— had never been in any doubt. The very fact that she obviously wanted that so badly perversely made Niccolo want to stay.

He shrugged. 'I am sure I have time to join you and your family for luncheon before I go.'

Daniella paled. 'I—'

'Well, of course you do.' Daniel Bell nodded his satisfaction with the arrangement. 'I'll take Mr D'Alessandro to the drawing room to meet Beatrice and Jeffrey while you go upstairs to shower and change, Daniella,' he added with a disapproving glance at her clothing.

Dani couldn't believe this was happening!

Niccolo couldn't really have any desire to prolong this torturous meeting, let alone further his acquaintance with any of the Bell family. Her grandfather's motive for the invitation was easy to guess; he just saw Niccolo—as he did any reasonable red-blooded man—as a possible father to the Bell heir. But she was sure that Niccolo's only intent in accepting the invitation was to make her feel uncomfortable.

How could she have been such a fool last Saturday? How could she not have known her fantasy lover was the arrogantly forceful Niccolo D'Alessandro?

Because she hadn't, that was how. Because she hadn't wanted to know. And now Niccolo was making her pay for that mistake.

One glance at Niccolo's face was enough to tell her how much he was enjoying her discomfort. Those dark eyes were glittering with mockery, those sculptured lips quirked into a derisive smile.

It was a self-satisfied smile that she wanted to wipe off those taunting lips!

'Perfect,' she accepted lightly. 'This way I'll be able to join you on your drive back to London, Niccolo, instead of spending hours sitting on an overcrowded train later this evening.'

Her gaze met his in glittering challenge. His expression didn't alter, but those dark, dark eyes took on a glitter as intense as her own. 'It would be my pleasure,' he finally said curtly.

Like hell it would, Dani thought happily. The last thing she wanted was to spend three hours in the confines of a car with Niccolo, but the fact that she knew he didn't want to spend those three hours with her, either, meant she intended doing exactly that.

And she'd thought *he* was being perverse! Feeling as they did about each other, they would probably both end up with indigestion from trying to eat lunch together, followed by three hours of awkward silence on the drive back to London.

But it would be worth it, Dani decided stubbornly, if only to show Niccolo that she had no intention of feeling guilty for what had happened last weekend. That she didn't care about his opinion of her.

Even if she did…

Just seeing Niccolo again, remembering the intimacies they had shared, was enough to show her that leaving London so hastily the previous weekend had achieved nothing. Seeing Niccolo again today only made her ache to repeat the experience.

It was at complete odds with the aversion Dani had felt towards physical relationships after her brief marriage to Philip, but she only had to look at Niccolo, at the broad width of his shoulders, his flat stomach and tapered thighs, to want him all over again.

But maybe she should tell him exactly what he was letting himself in for by accepting her grandfather's invitation to eat with them.

She broke away from the intensity of his gaze. 'Grandfather, would you mind very much if I just have a brief word with Niccolo in private? I promise I will point him in the direction of the sitting room as soon as we've finished talking,' she assured him as she saw her grandfather was about to protest.

'If you really must,' he allowed tightly, but he looked most displeased by this change in his arrangements.

It was a displeasure Dani refused to back down from. 'I really must,' she said firmly.

Her grandfather shot her one last narrow-eyed glare before turning to Niccolo. 'Don't let my granddaughter keep you out here too long,' he advised, before turning to stride stiff-backed into the house.

Dani waited only long enough for him to be safely out of earshot before turning back to Niccolo. 'What do you think you're doing?' she demanded fiercely.

Niccolo had been expecting this—had known from the outset that Daniella did not want him to accept the invitation to lunch; it was the very reason he had accepted!

'Politely accepting an invitation to luncheon with your family, I thought.'

'Why?'

He gave a humourless smile. 'It has obviously not occurred to you that I have driven for almost three hours this morning and would appreciate something to eat and drink before repeating the journey.'

Her eyes narrowed to green slits. 'You don't have to do that here—you could find any number of suitable places to eat on your way back to London.'

Niccolo gave an unconcerned shrug. 'I choose to do so here.'

Daniella shook her head. 'You'll regret it.'

Niccolo became very still as he looked down at her with hooded eyes. 'Are you threatening me, Daniella?'

She gave another shake of her head, her smile as humourless as the one he had given her seconds ago. 'I'm trying to warn you. The Bells, although you haven't yet had the chance to witness it, are your typical twenty-first-century dysfunctional family.'

Niccolo's mouth quirked. 'In what way?'

'In every way,' Dani said impatiently, knowing he wasn't taking this conversation seriously at all. 'My mother runs the house and gardens with grace and style. My father is a very successful trainer of racehorses—'

'And you, Daniella?' Niccolo taunted. 'Eleni tells me that you are a *very successful* interior designer.'

'So they say,' Dani confirmed, choosing to take his words at face value and ignore the sarcasm. 'But the truth of the matter is that my mother and father do not own Wiverley Hall and the stables; my grandfather does. And it is something that he never lets his son and daughter-in-law, or his disappointment of a granddaughter, ever forget.'

Niccolo looked at her searchingly, doubting for a moment that Daniella could be sincere in her warning. Admittedly Niccolo had only met Daniel Bell for a few minutes, and he was sure that Daniella knew her grandfather much better than he did, but the scenario she presented sounded a little extreme.

'In what way is he disappointed with his granddaughter?'

Daniella gave the ghost of a smile. 'I might have known you would pick up on that part of the statement. Probably because you share that disappointment…'

Disappointment was the last emotion Niccolo felt towards Daniella. He wasn't yet sure what emotions he *did* feel for her, but he was pretty sure disappointment was not amongst them.

'Do not change the subject, Daniella,' he advised harshly.

'I've been married and divorced, and all without producing the Bell heir,' she told him flatly. 'An unforgivable omission as far as Grandfather Bell is concerned.'

Dani regretted having even started this conversation; her grandfather's feelings towards her and her parents were none of Niccolo's business.

'Never mind—ten minutes in the company of the Bell family and you'll see exactly what I mean,' she said. 'Come into the house and I'll show you where the drawing room is—let me go, Niccolo!' she gasped as he suddenly reached out and grasped her arm.

He looked at her intently for several long, deliberate seconds before slowing releasing her. 'This conversation is not over, Daniella,' he warned softly.

As far as Dani was concerned it should never have begun!

But she didn't have any more time to argue about it now; she had to get herself quickly showered and changed before returning downstairs. The less time she left Niccolo alone with her parents—and with her obviously matchmaking grandfather—the better. Given the chance, her grandfather, just like her father with one of his horses, was likely to ask Niccolo for his complete pedigree!

'I did try to warn you,' Daniella sighed, as she sat beside Niccolo in the car later that afternoon and he drove them both back to London.

Yes, she had, Niccolo acknowledged ruefully. But even without that warning it would have been all too easy for him to pick up on the undercurrents of emotion running beneath the polite conversation as the five of them ate lunch together. Neither did Niccolo need to ask why Daniella was making further apologies now.

'You did,' he allowed. 'But that warning did not include the fact that your grandfather would be under the misapprehension that I am a prospective suitor for your hand in marriage,' he drawled.

The older man's barrage of questions about Niccolo's family and D'Alessandro business interests had bordered on rudeness. A fact Beatrice and Jeffrey Bell had also been aware of, if the way they had constantly tried to silence the older man was anything to go by.

Daniella turned to him. 'Don't take it personally, Niccolo; my grandfather considers any man under the age of sixty as being "a prospective suitor", as you so eloquently put it.'

Niccolo wasn't sure he altogether liked the image that statement conjured up. He and Daniella might be completely unsuited to each other, but the thought of some other faceless man making love with her in the way that he had was not a pleasant one.

He scowled. 'Why?'

Dani gave Niccolo a hard look, but could read nothing from his —deliberately?—bland expression. 'I told you—Grandfather is very big on continuing the Bell family line,' she dismissed with forced lightness.

Lunch had been as embarrassing as she had imagined it might be, with her grandfather asking Niccolo increasingly personal questions, and her parents doing their best to laugh it off. It hadn't helped that halfway through the meal her grandfather had made a scathing comment about Dani's 'friend Eleni'. And then he'd added insult to injury and remained completely unapologetic when Niccolo had frostily informed him that Eleni was his sister.

Her grandfather really was the most obnoxious man.

What Niccolo had thought of them all Dani had no idea. And she didn't particularly want to know, either!

'Don't look so worried, Niccolo,' she teased. 'I can assure you that I've told my grandfather repeatedly that I have no intention of marrying again.'

Niccolo raised dark brows. 'Was your first experience of marriage so awful, then?'

Awful? Traumatic better described it!

'Oh, yes.' She grimaced.

'Why?'

'I don't believe that's any of your business, Niccolo,' she snapped, too aware of him for comfort in the close confines of the car. Those brief few seconds of triumph she had felt earlier at wrong-footing him had been completely nullified by this self-imposed torture.

In fact, Dani wasn't sure *she* wasn't the one suffering the most discomfort from the arrangement, as Niccolo seemed his normal confidently relaxed self!

The previous mild interest Niccolo had felt towards Daniella's marriage became something much more at her blank refusal to discuss it.

Of course it was a personal matter—very personal—but the marriage had been of very short duration and had taken place two years ago now; surely long enough ago for Daniella to be able to talk about it dispassionately? Unless she still had feelings for her ex-husband....

It was strange, but after years of complete uninterest where Daniella Bell was concerned, Niccolo now found himself wanting to know everything he could about her. Perhaps because the Daniella he had thought he knew— and disapproved of—as Eleni's friend was a complete contradiction to the woman who had made love with him so passionately and unselfishly last weekend.

No matter how he tried, no matter how many times Daniella herself told him it was better for him to do so, Niccolo could not forget the woman in the gold gown. Or that Daniella and the woman in the gold gown were one and the same...

'And If I choose to make it my business?' he challenged her now.

'My advice is, *don't*!' she told him fiercely. 'Go back to Venice, Niccolo, and just forget any of this ever happened.'

That had been precisely his intention before he had spoken to Daniella today. But the more Daniella repeated that advice the less inclined Niccolo was to take it.

He drew in a harsh breath. 'I ask you again, Daniella— will *you* be able to do so?'

Never, came the unequivocal answer, Dani acknowledged heavily.

If her experience with Philip had soured her towards marriage for life, then her night with Niccolo had ruined her chances of ever taking another lover. That time with Niccolo had been so totally perfect that she knew anything else—anyone else—would always be second best.

She sighed. 'Does that really matter, Niccolo, when the two of us intend going back to our normal habit of ensuring that we see as little of each other as possible?'

'You do not think that our night together is reason enough for us to explore this...relationship further?'

She gave a choked laugh. 'The fact that you hesitated in even calling it a relationship should be answer enough!'

'I hesitated simply because I do not know what else to call it!' he growled. 'Damn it, Daniella, we both know that we found pleasure together that night.'

She closed her eyes to block out the image of his fiercely angry face, quickly opening them again as images of that night—being completely naked in Niccolo's arms, the beautiful strength of his perfectly proportioned body—instantly overwhelmed her.

'Have dinner with me this evening.'

'No!' she protested instantly, her hands clenching into such tight fists that her nails dug into her palms. 'No, Niccolo,' she repeated more calmly. 'We made a mistake; let's not compound it by trying to create something out of nothing.'

Niccolo had found her grandfather's interest both in his family and his financial affairs bordering on offensive earlier, but Daniella couldn't have shown him any more clearly that *she* had absolutely no interest in either of those things.

Intriguing.

He knew he was considered extremely eligible, but Niccolo didn't delude himself into believing his personality and looks had too much to do with that. Rather it was the D'Alessandro name and millions that gave him his eligible status. Dozens of women had pursued him with those things solely in mind.

But now Daniella was making it more than obvious that neither his name, money, or indeed he himself interested her!

'We will not know whether or not there is a basis on

which to create something until we have…explored the possibilities,' he said slowly.

Her mouth quirked. 'Until we've gone to bed together again, you mean?'

Was that what he had in mind? Possibly, Niccolo allowed grimly. And was that so unreasonable? Did Daniella have no curiosity herself to know whether or not they could recreate that one perfect night together? Did she feel none of the heated desire that churned just below the surface of their every conversation, their every glance? Had she not felt the same jolt of awareness he had just now, when he'd merely touched her arm?

'Are you not the least bit curious to know, Daniella?' he felt compelled to demand huskily.

Of course she was, Dani admitted privately. Only someone who was as blasé about lovemaking as Niccolo had earlier implied that she was could possibly remain immune to that curiosity.

But that curiosity, that daring, had already landed her in this impossible situation; to repeat it, with both of them aware of exactly who the other was, would be the height of stupidity.

'Not in the least, Niccolo,' she lied, with a brightness she was far from feeling, knowing by the angry tightening of Niccolo's mouth that her response had succeeded in alienating him. 'Now, if you don't mind, I think I would like to take a nap before we reach London.' She pointedly closed her eyes on the stony disapproval she could see in his face.

But she was far too aware of his brooding presence beside her for the next two hours to sleep, and her relief was immense when she realised that the increase in traffic and noise meant that they had finally reached their destination.

She opened her eyes to look around her. 'My apartment is—'

'I know where your apartment is, Daniella,' Niccolo gritted, the last two hours of silence having grated unbearably on his already frayed temper.

He desperately wanted to shake Daniella—wanted to physically pick her up and shake her until her teeth rattled.

His only reason for seeking her out today had been to clear the air between them, to somehow come to some sort of understanding that would enable them to meet again in future—as they were sure to do because Eleni was Daniella's best friend—without awkwardness.

But seeing Daniella again, speaking with her, had somehow achieved the opposite effect!

Dani sensed Niccolo was far from happy. Who could possibly have guessed so many complications would arise from what had at the time seemed so uncomplicated? *Come and enjoy the anonymity of a masked Venetian festival,* Eleni had invited her. *Take a lover, if you want one—at a Venetian festival it is allowed.*

Admittedly, Dani doubted that Eleni had intended for her to take Niccolo as that lover, and Dani knew now that any lover would have been a mistake.

Yet Niccolo's reaction to that night was to suggest repeating it—and Dani had spent the last two hours fighting against accepting that invitation!

Her body actually ached from the tension of remaining unmoving in the car beside him. Her jaw ached from the effort it had taken not to speak. And the closer they had got to London, to their parting, the harder it had been for her to remain silent and still.

'Thank you,' she muttered now, as Niccolo parked his car outside her apartment building.

'Daniella—'

'No, Niccolo. Don't say anything else—please!' she exclaimed, before turning to open the car door and scramble outside onto the pavement, immediately breathing in deep lungfuls of the late summer air in an effort to calm her rapidly racing pulse.

Everything looked as it normally did outside her apartment building. People strolling in the early evening sunshine in the park opposite. The ice-cream shop open across the street. One of her neighbours walking his dog.

Only she was different, it seemed.

And perhaps Niccolo a little, too…

Nothing, she realised emotionally, was ever going to be quite the same again…

'Daniella?'

She turned slightly confused eyes to look at Niccolo as he came to stand beside her after placing her overnight bag—all she had taken to Wiverley Hall as she kept some clothes there—on the pavement at her feet.

God, he looked good, she acknowledged achingly. His overlong hair appeared as dark as ebony in the sunlight, and his swarthy features were softened by that light too; deep brown eyes appeared almost golden, high cheekbones less hard, and his mouth—that pleasurably tormenting mouth!—had relaxed into a slightly enquiring smile.

She must not weaken now!

She straightened abruptly, her mouth set, green gaze direct. 'It was kind of you to drive me back to London,' she told him stiffly as she extended her hand.

Niccolo's breath caught in his throat as he looked down at the slenderness of that hand.

Daniella thought to part from him as if he were just any casual acquaintance who had given her a lift to her home? She believed that she could dismiss him, and the intimacy they had shared, so easily?

'Oh, no, Daniella,' he snarled, ignoring that hand to reach out, his hands planted firmly on the slenderness of her waist, and draw her towards him. 'You do not dismiss me so easily!' And with that his head lowered and his mouth took fierce possession of hers.

Niccolo's eyes closed instinctively, shutting out her startled expression as his mouth began to taste, to savour hers.

She tasted like the woman in gold!

She felt the same!

She *was* the same…

Niccolo growled low in his throat as, with a soft groan of surrender, her lips parted to deepen the kiss, and he drew her body close into his to mould her softness against his much harder contours.

His body leapt with remembered, renewed desire, heat rising rapidly between them as he restlessly caressed the curve of her spine, holding her firmly against him so that she could feel his throbbing response.

He wanted her.

Now.

Wanted to feel her naked beneath him as he plunged

deep inside her, as his hardness stroked rhythmically against her arousal. Wanted to once again feel her heat, her passion, as she convulsed around him in ecstasy.

How could Daniella even think of denying them that pleasure—?

Dani wrenched her mouth away from Niccolo's to look up at him with dark, slightly bruised-looking green eyes, her breathing ragged as she pushed against his chest to be released.

'Let me go, Niccolo,' she told him shakily as he still held her tightly against him. 'Let me go *now*!' she repeated fiercely, her eyes glittering angrily.

He blinked once at her vehemence before narrowing his gaze questioningly. His arms slowly fell back to his sides to allow Dani to step back.

She was trembling, shaking—more shaken, more aroused than she could ever allow Niccolo to know.

God knew what would have happened if they hadn't been standing on a public London street! Her jaw tightened and she looked up at him challengingly. 'What was that supposed to prove?'

'I did not set out to prove anything, Daniella. What it did prove is that you are not as immune to me as you claim to be.'

She breathed raggedly. 'You—!'

'It also proved that you will not find it so easy to forget our evening together as you think it will,' he continued ruthlessly.

'Neither will you!' Dani retorted.

'I never claimed I would forget it, Daniella,' he reminded her softly.

No, he hadn't, had he? she thought. In fact, Niccolo had been so affected by their lovemaking last weekend that he had spent the last few days searching for the woman in the gold gown.

Well, now he had found her. Only, as Dani had no intention of becoming Niccolo's latest mistress in a no doubt long line of mistresses, it was up to her to put a stop to this once and for all. Even at the risk of damaging her friendship with Eleni.

She forced a deliberately mocking smile to her lips. 'I really do hate to dent your inflated ego, Niccolo, but our lovemaking really wasn't that memorable, and I can assure you I am going to have absolutely no problem whatsoever in forgetting both it and you!'

To her chagrin, her claim only made Niccolo smile. Widely. Confidently. 'Have you ever heard the saying "the lady doth protest too much"…?'

'Of course I've heard it,' she snapped. 'It just doesn't happen to apply in this case.'

'No?' he pressed.

'No!' Dani scowled fiercely.

'Very well.' He nodded, those sculptured lips still curved into a mocking smile. 'I will be back in London at the end of next month, Daniella. Four weeks from now.'

'Of what interest can that possibly be to me?'

'If your lack of interest is genuine, then it will be of little relevance,' Niccolo allowed. 'But if, as I suspect, your body still burns with the same desire as mine, then it may be of great interest—'

'God, you're unbelievably arrogant!' Dani cut in.

Niccolo knew that his arrogance was a part of his nature,

that it was part and parcel of being the head of the D'Alessandro family and business. But when he talked of the desire that burned between himself and Daniella he knew he was not speaking out of arrogance, but fact. Just now had proved as much. And perhaps the month until he and Daniella could meet again would give her time to realise the truth of that too.

He sincerely hoped that it would!

He gave an elegant shrug. 'I am merely being more truthful, both to myself and you, than you appear to be.'

'You just want to find yourself a convenient mistress for whenever you're in London!'

Niccolo refused to rise to her deliberate attempt at insulting him. 'And what sort of mistress do you think you would make, Daniella?'

'A very unaccommodating one.'

He smiled at the obvious truth of that remark; anyone less like the warm and, yes, accommodating women he had taken as mistresses in the past he had yet to meet!

'I'm glad you find this so funny, Niccolo,' she continued as she saw and obviously misunderstood that smile. The impatience in her tone told him she found it the exact opposite of amusing. 'What do you think Eleni would have to say about all this?'

Niccolo's humour faded, and his mouth tightened at what was an obvious ploy on Daniella's part to halt this conversation by mentioning his sister.

Eleni had had plenty to say to him earlier that morning, before he'd set out for Gloucestershire, leaving Niccolo in no doubt whatsoever that if he intended harming Dani in any way he would have Eleni to answer to.

'What is between us does not concern Eleni,' he stated flatly.

'There is absolutely *nothing* between us, Niccolo!' Dani denied desperately, her unfair use of Eleni as a weapon having failed utterly. 'This—whatever it was—is over.'

'Keep telling yourself that, Daniella,' he drawled as he took the car keys from his trouser pocket before moving around to the driver's side of the car. 'Who knows? By the time I return in four weeks' time you might even have convinced yourself into believing it.' He raised one mocking eyebrow. 'I will then have the pleasure of proving otherwise.'

Dani opened her mouth to tell him exactly what he could do with his *pleasure*, but the words died on her lips as he slid smoothly behind the wheel of the car and closed the door behind him before turning on the ignition.

Arrogant, arrogant man, she muttered to herself in frustration as she watched Niccolo drive away.

It could be four weeks until she saw him again, four years or four decades, and she would not—she *could not*—give in to the desire Niccolo ignited inside her with just a look!

CHAPTER FIVE

'DID you decide that you could not, after all, wait the full four weeks until my return to London this weekend?'

Niccolo's surprise of a few minutes ago, when his secretary had come into his Venetian office and told him of Daniella Bell's presence in the outer room, was completely under control now as he sat behind the width of his imposing leather-topped oak desk and looked at the slenderness of Daniella's back where she stood across the room from him, gazing out of the window at the busy Grand Canal below.

He had stood up when she entered the room, and indicated for her to take a seat across the desk from his. But instead of doing so Daniella had moved to the huge window, her back remaining firmly towards him as she gazed out at the beauty that was Venice in September, with the weak sun bathing the buildings and the water in a soft amber glow.

Niccolo had seen that view dozens of times in his lifetime, both before his father died and then more since he had taken over this office as his own, and he knew exactly how mystical, how beautiful Venice looked as it stretched majestically into the hazy distance.

But Daniella had been in the room for at least five minutes now, and so far had not spoken a word….

'Daniella?' he prompted impatiently, when she did not even respond to the deliberate provocation of his remark.

It was three and a half weeks since he had last seen her. Three and a half weeks during which he had not forgotten a single thing about her or the evening they had made love so beautifully. Three and a half weeks during which he had longed to return to London, but forced himself not to do so to give Daniella time. Time, he had hoped, to discover she wanted him as much as he still wanted her.

When Melina had told him Daniella was here, waiting outside to see him, Niccolo had believed that to be the case and had been filled with expectation. But Daniella's behaviour since entering the room—her silence, the fact that she had barely glanced at him before moving to stand in front of the window with her back towards him—did not fill him with the same confidence.

But by the same token, she could have not have flown to Venice, sought him out at his office, without good reason…

She was dressed more formally than he would have expected. Her black suit was expertly tailored and matched with a cream silk blouse; her slender legs and feet were bare in black court shoes. The formality of her clothing implied this was more of a business appointment than a social call.

'Daniella, your silence is becoming intolerable!' he rasped, his movements restless as he stood up.

Dani was aware of Niccolo behind her in the room, just as she had been aware for several minutes of his rising impatience at her silence.

She hadn't meant for it to be this way. Had intended coming to Venice to see Niccolo, and stating confidently and calmly exactly how she intended things to be between them in future, then returning to her hotel to spend the night there before flying back to England tomorrow.

But one glance at Niccolo when she'd entered the room—just one heart-stopping look at his ruggedly handsome face and lithely muscular body in the lightweight grey suit and pristine white shirt with its neatly knotted grey tie—and Dani had felt her throat close up and her mouth go completely dry, making it impossible for her to force a single word past her lips.

Niccolo was perfectly correct. This silence could not continue!

She straightened her shoulders and forced herself to turn, slightly disconcerted to find he had moved from behind the desk and was now standing only feet away, but determined to stand firm and say what needed to be said.

'Okay,' she breathed huskily. 'This is the way it's going to be. I will continue to live in England, but you may visit whenever you are in London—'

'Stop right there!' he cut in icily. 'Daniella.' His voice softened as he saw her pallor. 'You are discussing a possible relationship between the two of us as if it were a business arrangement,' he chided gently.

Dani blinked, confused for a moment, until she realised exactly what Niccolo was saying. 'You thought I was discussing the two of us having an *affair*?' she said with a frown.

He looked nonplussed. 'What else—?'

'No, Niccolo,' she interrupted. 'You have it all wrong. *I* have it all wrong,' she corrected agitatedly. 'I'm not doing this very well at all.' She groaned, pushing the silky swathe of her fiery-red hair back impatiently. 'I'm a bit flustered, Niccolo. I'm sorry.' She looked at him appealingly.

Niccolo returned that gaze searchingly, having already noted the paleness of Daniella's cheeks, the dark shadows beneath those anguished green eyes, the way her hands were tightly clenched together in front of her until the knuckles showed white.

'Perhaps you should sit down?' he said slowly. 'I will ask Melina to bring us some coffee—'

'No, not coffee!' Daniella grimaced in apology for her sharpness. 'Tea would be nice,' she accepted.

Niccolo didn't bother ringing for his secretary, but instead strode over to open the door and make his request verbally. Much to Melina's surprise, he acknowledged ruefully, before closing the door and turning back to Daniella.

She hadn't moved from in front of the window, and she looked incredibly slender standing there, bathed in the soft September sunlight like a slender reed topped with flame. A slender, vulnerable reed…

'I really do think you should sit down, Daniella,' he pressed gently. 'Before you fall down,' he added more firmly, when she looked up at him slightly dazed.

Dani swallowed hard, knowing Niccolo was right. At this moment her legs *were* feeling more than a little shaky. But she had been so anxious to establish the parameters between them that she had totally missed an explanation as to why those parameters were needed in the first place.

'Thank you,' she accepted, before moving jerkily to sit down on the chair in front of his desk. 'Won't you sit down, too?' she invited, hoping that the formality of their sitting on either side of his imposing oak desk might make this easier for her.

Although she somehow doubted it!

She hadn't given herself time to think once the decision to come to Venice to talk to Niccolo had been made—had simply booked her flight and turned up at his office ten minutes ago, asking to see him.

But being here, face to face with Niccolo like this, it was all too easy to realise the enormity of what she was doing. To realise just how difficult all this was going to be.

It might have helped if she had got her thoughts into some sort of order before coming here, for one thing; at least then she might not have made such a complete muddle of things.

In her haste to get it over and done with, it seemed she had completely misled Niccolo into believing she had come here to work out the terms of an affair with him. When in fact the reason for her visit couldn't be any further from the truth....

Niccolo moved to sit behind his desk and studied Daniella in concern. She didn't look well. In fact, he was sure she had lost weight since he'd last saw her. If just coming here to see him had made Daniella ill, then she was right; no matter what he might have hoped to the contrary, there could never be a relationship between the two of them.

'Don't look so worried, Niccolo,' she murmured rue-fully as she saw his look of concern. 'I haven't been feeling too well the last couple of weeks, but I'm not ill. Well—not ill, exactly. Can you really not guess the reason I'm here, Niccolo?'

No, he really couldn't.

And he was feeling too perplexed, too disturbed by this unexpected visit to play guessing games with her!

'Tell me,' he ordered.

Her eyes suddenly looked huge in the pallor of her face, her cheekbones standing out starkly above hollow cheeks. 'The truth is, Niccolo, that I flew over from England this morning to—' She broke off as Melina, after the briefest of knocks, entered carrying a tray of tea things. Daniella looked up to smile her thanks at the older woman as she placed the tray in front of her on the desk.

Niccolo barely held his impatience in check until his secretary had left the room. 'Pour it,' he invited Daniella. 'You look as if you need it,' he added with a frown as she sat forward to pick up the teapot. 'Has something happened to Eleni?'

'No!' Daniella gave him a startled look. 'Oh, no, Niccolo, you mustn't think that.' She handed him one of the cups of tea before putting a liberal amount of sugar in her own cup and taking a grateful sip. She sat back with a sigh, a little of the colour returning to her cheeks. 'No one is ill, Niccolo. I— The fact of the matter is—the truth is that I—I'm pregnant, Niccolo! Over a month pregnant to be exact,' she added shakily.

Niccolo stared at her uncomprehendingly.

Dani's eyes were wide with distress as she looked across at him searchingly, knowing what a shock this must be for him.

What a shock it had been for her, too, yesterday morning, when she had finally plucked up the courage to use the pregnancy testing kit she had purchased from a chemist the day before.

She hadn't even realised she had missed a period until two days ago—had been keeping herself so busy, her thoughts carefully channelled in an effort not to think of Niccolo, that she had completely omitted to notice that her body wasn't functioning as meticulously like clockwork as it usually did.

Even once she had realised she had missed a period she had dismissed the idea that she might be pregnant as ridiculous; surely it was an old wives' tale that it only took the once?

Apparently it wasn't!

Not convinced by the first test she had done, Dani had used the second test in the box. That had shown a positive result too. Still hopeful that she might have got a faulty testing kit, she had made an emergency appointment to see her doctor, at which point he had calmly and kindly explained to her that neither of the tests was faulty, that she was indeed in the early stages of pregnancy.

Which was when complete panic had set in!

No doubt her grandfather would be thrilled by the news, but Dani's first instinct had been to run. Her second and third instinct too! As fast and as far from Niccolo as she could possibly go.

But she had very quickly realised the futility of doing that. She couldn't just disappear, any more than she could carry on running for ever—and certainly not once the baby was born. She had to have some means of supporting the baby, as well as herself, and London was where her business was established. Besides, Eleni was far too astute, and knew Dani far too well, to ever accept her just disappearing like that. By the same token, if Dani remained in London, from the timing alone Eleni would know that Niccolo was the father of Dani's baby. And while Dani didn't doubt her friend's love for her, the love and loyalty Eleni also felt towards her brother would put her in an intolerable position.

So, as running away wasn't really an option, and keeping the truth from Niccolo was virtually an impossibility, Dani had decided she had no choice but to come to Venice and tell Niccolo herself of his impending fatherhood.

So far there had been no response to her news except the shocked widening of his eyes and his continued silence. But knowing Niccolo as she did, that didn't mean there wasn't plenty going on behind those unfathomable brown eyes. Once Niccolo recovered from the shock of her announcement he was definitely going to have several things to say on the subject.

She moistened dry lips. 'Could you just say something, Niccolo?' she asked. 'Anything.' She grimaced. 'Just don't keep looking at me in that stunned way.'

But stunned was exactly how Niccolo felt!

Stunned. Shocked. Numbed.

Daniella had just told him— Had said—

He swallowed hard, realising as he did so that he had forgotten to breathe for the last minute. His normally astute brain had for once ground to a halt.

'Niccolo, please!' Daniella pleaded at his continued silence.

Niccolo knew he had to do something. Say something. He just had no idea what!

He finally drew in a ragged breath before speaking. 'Have you eaten lunch?'

Daniella blinked. 'I— What?' She stared at him in disbelief.

Niccolo breathed out. Then in again. That soft rising and falling of his chest was the only thing that seemed normal to him at this moment.

'You said you flew over from England this morning,' he pointed out evenly. 'I wondered if you had eaten since your arrival?'

Dani continued to stare at him. She had just told Niccolo that she was pregnant, with his child, and all he could do was ask her if she had eaten lunch?

She had expected disbelief—goodness knows she had expected that! But she had also expected that disbelief to be quickly followed by anger, and then Niccolo's arrogant demands for what he wanted.

If anyone had asked her what his first words would be after she told him of her pregnancy, her answer certainly wouldn't have been an invitation to lunch!

'Niccolo, did you hear what I just said?'

'Of course I heard you!' he snapped as he stood up abruptly to move around to the front of the desk, a nerve pulsing in his tightly clenched jaw as he looked down at her with glittering dark eyes. 'Daniella, you have had time to come to terms with your pregnancy; you must have known for several days at least—'

'Twenty-four hours,' she corrected softly, infinitely more comfortable with his explosion than with his silence, her chin rising challengingly as she added, 'I only found out myself yesterday, Niccolo.'

His eyes narrowed. 'That is something, I suppose,' he allowed. 'Have you seen a doctor? Are you well? You look to me as if you have lost weight, not gained it!' he accused.

This was more like the Niccolo D'Alessandro Dani knew!

Some of the tension left her shoulders and she relaxed back in the chair. 'I saw my doctor yesterday.' She nodded. 'And I'm very well.' She gave a tremulous smile. 'Weight loss can be perfectly natural in the early stages of—of pregnancy.'

She couldn't believe she was sitting here discussing her condition so calmly with Niccolo—still had trouble believing that she was pregnant at all.

Niccolo was right. She had lost weight these last few weeks. She had put her loss of appetite and extreme tiredness, the fact that food didn't even appeal to her, down to her stress over Niccolo's imminent return and her near obsession with keeping herself too busy to think about what she was going to say to him when he did.

It was natural to find food unappetising during the first few months of pregnancy, her doctor had assured her yesterday. And it was equally natural to feel tired and nauseous. She hadn't felt the latter yet, but there was still plenty of time for that!

'We will go out to lunch,' Niccolo stated. 'You need to eat, and we can discuss this further once you have done so.'

'Oh, but—'

'Do not argue with me on this, Daniella,' he warned tightly, his hands clenched into fists at his sides. 'You must eat, and I—I need a few minutes in which to process what you have told me,' he added harshly.

Yes, Dani could see that he did. She even understood why he did. She would just have preferred not to make a social occasion out of it by the two of them actually going out to lunch together.

She might have muddled things earlier, but she did

know how she wanted this to go. She had come here to tell Niccolo of her pregnancy, to assure him that he could have visiting access at any time he liked once the baby was born, and then she would return to London and get on with her life until the birth.

She should have known Niccolo would change the order of things—as he was doing so now, by insisting on taking her out to lunch!

Niccolo watched as first her understanding for his dilemma, followed by a look of stubborn resolve and then frowning determination flickered across Daniella's expressive face.

The first he understood. It had to be obvious to even the most casual observer—and Daniella was hardly that— that he was totally stunned by the news of Daniella's pregnancy.

The second he also understood—he already knew how stubbornly self-reliant Daniella could be when she chose, and he suddenly remembered her words earlier: 'I will continue to live in England, but you may visit whenever you are in London!'

Her look of determination was also easily understood— Daniella would not give in meekly to any demands he might choose to make concerning the child she carried.

But she would give in.

Oh, yes, Daniella would give in.

Eventually.

Because it was his child as well as hers, and Niccolo had no intention of giving in meekly to any demands she might choose to make concerning their child, either!

* * *

'This is nice,' Dani murmured as she looked around the quiet bistro Niccolo had brought her to, his hand having lightly but firmly gripped her arm as he guided her well away from the tourist-busy St Mark's Square to this small family-owned restaurant that overlooked one of the narrower canals. The owner had greeted Niccolo by name before showing them to one of the tables by the open windows.

'Eat, Daniella,' Niccolo instructed as the owner deposited breadsticks on the table, along with their menus.

Dani ignored his order and instead picked up the menu to use as a shield as she shot Niccolo frowning glances. He had barely spoken on the ten-minute walk here along the path-sided canals, but she knew from the slight pallor beneath his naturally swarthy complexion that this was only a temporary respite—that in actual fact Niccolo did have plenty to say, and was just choosing the moment when he would say it. Probably he would get started once she had eaten, as he seemed so determined to get some food down her!

'Stop thinking so much, Daniella, and instead choose what you would like for lunch.'

Dani looked up, not fooled for a moment by the pleasantness of his tone.

'Niccolo—'

'I believe there are certain foods that pregnant women have to avoid?' he prompted lightly.

'Smoked meat and fish, pâtés, soft cheeses, uncooked eggs,' she confirmed distractedly, having received a list of dos and don'ts from the doctor yesterday. 'But—'

'Then perhaps you would like the linguine with mushrooms and chicken?'

'Niccolo—'

'We will order our food before continuing this conversation, Daniella.' His tone was steely, uncompromising.

She drew in a breath to reply, but was prevented from further argument by the arrival of the proprietor to take their order, and waited until they were alone again before carefully placing her hands down on the red and white checked cloth that covered the small, square table to lean forward and look Niccolo directly in the eye. 'I do sincerely sympathise with the shock this has been to you—'

'Do you?' Niccolo drawled, perfectly relaxed as he leant back in his chair.

'Well, of course I do,' She groaned. 'It isn't every day you learn you're going to become a father.'

'No,' he conceded dryly. 'But it is not so much of a shock now as it originally was,' he admitted, that dark gaze lazily assessing. 'In fact, now that I have...adjusted to the idea, I find that the prospect of having a son or daughter is rather a pleasant one.'

Yes, Niccolo had certainly recovered from his earlier speechlessness, Dani acknowledged uneasily. And as she knew only too well, a totally self-possessed Niccolo was a force to be reckoned with.

What on earth had made her imagine that telling Niccolo herself about her pregnancy was the easiest option? What had possessed her to think that she could come here and tell Niccolo about the baby and that he would then just calmly allow her to return to England to continue her pregnancy without any interference from him?

Because the almost complacent way in which he had said

that he found the idea of having a child a pleasant one certainly implied he didn't intend letting her escape that easily!

'Niccolo, I don't think you've quite understood what's going to happen here,' she told him. 'You are biologically going to become a father in around eight months' time, yes, but not—not a hands-on father. Not a permanent, day-to-day fixture in this child's life!' she added slightly desperately.

Niccolo shook his head and smiled, seeming totally unconcerned by the vehemence in Daniella's announcement. 'I think that it is *you* who does not understand, Daniella,' he contradicted her. 'The child you are carrying is a D'Alessandro. More than that, as my son or daughter, he or she will be the D'Alessandro heir.'

She nodded. 'I do understand that, Niccolo—'

'No, you obviously do not.' He sat forward to lean across the table, his face only inches from hers now. 'As soon as the arrangements can be made, Daniella, you and I will be married,' he stated.

And watched with a wicked pleasure as she recoiled in horror!

CHAPTER SIX

'MARRIED?' Dani repeated incredulously when she finally managed to recover enough from the shock of Niccolo's announcement to find her voice again. 'I have no intention of marrying you or anyone else, Niccolo!'

He straightened abruptly, dark eyes suddenly glacial above his hard cheekbones and rigidly set jaw. 'Believe me, Daniella, there is no question of your marrying anyone else *but* me,' he bit out tautly.

She shook her head. 'You or anyone else, Niccolo,' she repeated determinedly. 'I told you weeks ago that I will never marry again.'

'The circumstances were different then,' he said with quiet violence.

'I wasn't pregnant, you mean?' Dani nodded. 'But that changes nothing—'

'It changes *everything*!' Niccolo glared at her. 'I have told you. The child you carry is the D'Alessandro heir, and as such—'

'It's also the Bell heir,' she reminded him, with no small measure of disgust, already able to imagine how thrilled her grandfather was going to be by the news. He was so filled with his own self-importance he would probably imagine she had become pregnant just to satisfy his demand for a great-grandchild—

Oh, God.

She shot Niccolo an apprehensive glance even as the colour drained from her face. If Niccolo learnt of the contents of her grandfather's will, would he think she had deliberately arranged this pregnancy in order to safeguard her parents' future?

Remembering Eleni's fleeting suspicions of that possibility four weeks ago, after Dani and Niccolo had spent the evening together, Dani had the dreadful feeling that he just might….

But there was no reason why Niccolo should ever know about that clause in her grandfather's will. And even if he did learn of it, it wasn't as if she was asking him for anything, was it?

Except the Bell heir…

No!

One thing at a time, she reminded herself. One problem at a time. And she had enough of those already without thinking of ones that hadn't even arisen yet!

'Daniella, what is it?' Niccolo queried urgently as he watched her cheeks pale. 'Daniella, you will tell me what is wrong!' he demanded forcefully, totally frustrated with her complete intractability concerning the idea of a marriage between them.

Could she not see that it was the only solution? That he would settle for nothing less?

And what of Daniella's wants and needs? came the unbidden thought….

He thrust it aside. Daniella was pregnant—a time during which a woman's hormones and emotions reputedly made logical thought and decisions virtually impossible. The fact that she was pregnant with his child, that he wanted to marry her, surely made her decision never to marry again totally illogical?

Dani firmly closed her mind to thoughts of what Niccolo might or might not come to think of her pregnancy if he learnt of that clause in her grandfather's will. At the moment her main difficulty was getting it through to Niccolo that she was not, under any circumstances, going to marry him. Although she would be lying if she said that she hadn't felt a slight thrill, a frisson of excitement, when Niccolo had announced his intention of marrying her.

It hadn't been her immediate reaction, of course. Initially she had been absolutely horrified just at the mention of a marriage between the two of them—had never even considered that Niccolo would make such an offer.

Although perhaps she should have done...

Niccolo was Italian, and more than that he was a D'Alessandro—a member of a Venetian family steeped in honour and tradition; the idea that the D'Alessandro heir might be born out of wedlock, so to speak, was probably enough to send Niccolo's ancestors spinning in their graves!

She gave a rueful shake of her head. 'What is wrong, Niccolo, is that I don't want to marry you,' she stated baldly, grimacing as she saw the angry glitter of his eyes and the way his mouth tightened inflexibly. 'Be totally honest—it isn't what you really want, either, now, is it?' she added reasonably.

This was all too new to Niccolo for him to know *what* he wanted. Admittedly, for the last three and a half weeks he had been quietly contemplating—relishing!—the idea of the two of them beginning a relationship, but he could not in all honesty say that marriage had ever entered into any of those fantasies.

But now that it had…

The prospect of having Daniella as his wife was not an unpleasant one. And the thought of having her permanently in his bed, of the two of them making love whenever and wherever they pleased, was extremely exciting.

Besides, there was no question as to whether or not it was what either of them really wanted—their child needed two parents, and parents who lived together, so that the child did not become some sort of human ping-pong ball.

'It *is* what I want, Daniella,' he insisted.

'But it can't be!' Dani protested fiercely. 'Until a few weeks ago the two of us couldn't even be in the same room without arguing—so nothing new there, then.' She sighed ruefully as she realised that was exactly what they were doing now. 'Niccolo.' She reached out and placed her hand on his, instantly regretting the action as she felt an electrical charge of physical awareness tingle up her hand and along her arm. She snatched her hand away. 'I promise you I will not make it difficult for you to see your son or daughter whenever you wish—'

'That would be every day, then,' he cut in harshly. 'A promise you could not possibly keep if you reside in England and my own home is here in Venice.'

Impasse.

Coming here and telling Niccolo about the baby

couldn't solve that particular problem. But Dani would not allow herself to be browbeaten into marrying him.

Oh, she knew he was nothing like Philip—that Niccolo possessed none of the insecurity or mental imbalance that had become manifest in Philip so soon after their wedding. But the thought of being any man's wife again, of placing herself in that position of vulnerability, was complete anathema to her.

She doubted she would be able to make Niccolo understand any of that without totally explaining the nightmare of her first marriage to him. Unfortunately, that was something she did not intend doing.

'I'm sorry, Niccolo, but the whole idea of the two of us marrying is unthinkable to me.'

Why? Niccolo was puzzled, completely aware that only minutes ago, when Daniella had touched his arm so impulsively, she had been as physically aware of him as he had been of her since the night of Eleni's masquerade party.

Probably before that night, he allowed ruefully, having had plenty of time to think in the three and a half weeks since he had last seen her. One thing he had come to understand was that he had already been aware of Daniella Bell and how she had grown into a beautiful young woman since he had helped Eleni move to England six years ago.

It had been the fact that Daniella had been only eighteen, while Niccolo was already thirty-one, and that she was also Eleni's best friend, that had put up a barrier so that Niccolo had felt he could never pursue that attraction.

And so had begun the verbal battles between them that

had punctuated every one of their meetings during the last six years.

Until the night of Eleni's masquerade party….

That night of anonymity had wiped away all those barriers, had allowed him to appreciate her even if he hadn't recognised her as Daniella. He had simply seen her as a beautiful and mature woman.

Damn it, she was *his* woman.

Carrying *his* child.

He would not allow her to walk away from him!

His mouth firmed with resolution. 'I too am sorry, Daniella—because the idea of the two of us *not* marrying is unthinkable to *me*.'

Dani sighed, but was saved from making any immediate answer by the arrival of their food. Not that she had any appetite for it, but the interruption was welcome.

What were they going to do?

She lived and worked in London. Niccolo lived and worked here in Venice. Niccolo was insisting that they get married. And she was insisting that they wouldn't.

Maybe she should have just followed her first instinct and started running—and kept on going….

'Does Eleni know about the baby?' Niccolo asked as soon as the two of them were alone again.

Daniella froze in the action of sprinkling parmesan over her pasta.

'No, of course she doesn't,' she denied. 'No one else knows but the two of us. I— It didn't seem…right that I should tell anyone else before I had talked to you.'

He gave an abrupt inclination of his head. 'That is something, I suppose.'

She looked pained. 'Niccolo, I am trying to be fair.'

'Fair, perhaps,' he grated. 'I would prefer reasonable.'

'I'm trying to be reasonable, too—'

'You call refusing to marry your baby's father *reasonable*?' Niccolo accused harshly.

Tears swam in her beautiful green eyes. 'I'm sorry.' She hastily wiped away the tears before they could fall onto the paleness of her cheeks. 'I believe pregnant woman tend to be a little—over-emotional,' she whispered.

Niccolo felt like a complete heel now. He hadn't intended to make Daniella cry—hadn't intended to upset her at all—but she was just being so damned stubborn by continuing to refuse to marry him!

He closed his eyes briefly, but could still inwardly see her woebegone face and tear-wet lashes.

He appreciated that this couldn't have been easy for Daniella. That it had taken great courage for her to come here like this today and tell him of the baby. She could have had no idea how he would react to the news.

He was just so frustrated with her refusal to marry him!

It was pretty obvious she wasn't going to change her mind without a fight, either. A fight Niccolo didn't believe she was emotionally or physically equipped to deal with right now.

He raised his lids, his eyes widening as he saw that her face had a slightly green tinge to it. 'What is it?' he asked with immediate concern.

Dani swallowed hard. 'I don't think I should have put this much parmesan on my pasta….' The pungent odour of the cheese on the hot food was making her feel extremely nauseous.

Niccolo reached across the table to remove her plate and replace it with his own ungarnished pasta.

'Oh, but—'

'Just eat, Daniella,' he told her wearily. 'Eat, and then we will continue our conversation.'

Dani wasn't sure that the delay was going to make any difference to the situation, but once her stomach had stopped churning from the smell of the melting cheese she realised that she was actually quite hungry. Not surprising, really, when she had been too nervous earlier this morning at the thought of seeing Niccolo again—at what she had to tell him—to even think about eating any breakfast.

She did feel slightly better once she had eaten Niccolo's pasta, and a rather delicious dessert something like an English trifle. But if their conversation was going to continue along the same impossible lines Dani knew she was just as likely to lose it all again!

She ran her tongue nervously over her bottom lip. 'Niccolo—'

'Not here, Daniella,' he said, before turning to ask for the bill. 'We will continue our conversation at my home.'

Considering that home to Niccolo was the D'Alessandro palace, Dani didn't think she was going to find talking there any more comfortable than she had here.

Eleni had once shown Dani photographs of her family home: a tall, five-storeyed building with a boathouse below, slightly Arabian in style, with an extensive garden on the roof. A home fit for the princes the D'Alessandro men had once been.

Her child—her son or daughter—was descended from princes!

From priests and pirates too, of course, she remembered wryly, but she doubted if members of either of those professions had actually lived in the D'Alessandro palace.

'Will you be comfortable travelling by boat, or would you rather walk?' Niccolo asked once they were outside.

Eleni had once gone into raptures about the thrill of approaching the D'Alessandro palace by boat, waxing lyrical about how beautiful it was viewed from the water.

'Boat will be fine,' Dani accepted huskily.

This really was a completely different way of life, she thought as she sat in the back of the small motorboat Niccolo piloted out into the busy Grand Canal, where dozens of boats similar to this one, as well as water-taxis and the much more romantic gondolas, glided smoothly through the water.

But it was Niccolo himself who held her attention as he sat behind the wheel, the slight breeze ruffling the darkness of his overlong hair, those beautiful brown eyes narrowed in concentration as he easily manoeuvred the boat through the slightly choppy water created by the passing of other crafts.

It was the first time Dani had had a chance to really look at him without the nerve-racking barrier of telling him of her pregnancy between them. She felt her heart actually skipping a beat as she gazed hungrily at the rugged handsomeness of his face.

She had been infatuated with him at the age of fourteen. Had remained fascinated by him and then, after her marriage, had shied away from his raw sexuality. Well, her fascination had been ecstatically satisfied just a few weeks ago!

She couldn't help wondering what her answer would have been if she hadn't been pregnant. If Niccolo had come to London on the weekend, as promised, to ask if she had changed her mind about entering into a relationship with him.

Would she have continued to say no?

Or would she have said yes, and happily grabbed the days, weeks, possibly months of having Niccolo as her lover?

Sadly, she would never know the answer to that now.

'Why the sigh?'

Dani shook off her mood of despondency and looked up to find Niccolo glancing back at her. 'I was just thinking how lucky you are to live somewhere so beautiful,' she said mendaciously.

It took great effort for Niccolo not to point out that Venice could become her home too, if she would only say yes to his marriage proposal; however, a motorboat in the middle of a Venetian canal was not the ideal place in which to begin yet another argument between them.

'Yes, it is,' he agreed casually. 'And here is the D'Alessandro palace.' He kept one hand on the wheel as he pointed with the other to the pale terracotta-coloured building that had been his family home for generations. He couldn't help but be inwardly pleased by the look of pleasure that instantly lit Daniella's features as she turned to look at it, her eyes glowing, an excited flush to her cheeks, her beautiful, kissable mouth curved into a rapt smile.

'Oh, Niccolo, it's *wonderful*!' she breathed.

Niccolo slowed the boat to manoeuvre it into its mooring beneath the house, before turning to help Daniella step onto the paved walkway that led to a staircase up into the main part of the palace.

'Could you bring tea up to the drawing-room, Edoardo?' he asked his manservant as the other man came into the spacious hallway to greet them. Niccolo kept his amusement contained as the elderly man showed none of the surprise he was probably feeling at the return of his employer in the middle of the afternoon, with a beautiful redhead secured firmly at his side, and he kept a light hold on Daniella's arm.

Dani, accompanying Niccolo up the wide staircase to the first floor, had never seen such a beautiful house. The decorations were ornately gold, the lavish furniture obviously genuinely antique. Huge paintings hung on the walls, and a crystal chandelier was suspended from the high ceiling above them.

She followed Niccolo as he threw open tall doors that led into what was obviously the drawing room. The domed ceiling of this room held Dani's attention, painted with cherubs and maidens, with more ornate gold filigree work and yet another crystal chandelier also suspended above them.

Having grown up in Wiverley Hall she was, of course, used to big houses, but the D'Alessandro palace was in a class completely on its own; it was unbelievably magnificent in its opulence.

She gave a choked laugh. 'Eleni told me it was beautiful, but I had no idea…'

'Come and look at the view,' Niccolo encouraged huskily as he opened the doors out onto the balcony before turning to hold out his hand to her in invitation.

Dani stared at that hand, feeling suddenly shy with him, never having quite appreciated before how in other circumstances Niccolo might have been Prince D'Alessandro. But it was all too easy, in these grand surroundings, to imagine him as such—to recognise his innate air of command, to acknowledge him as the powerful and much-respected head of the D'Alessandro family.

Niccolo was offering to share all of this with her, to make her his wife, the mother of his child—children…? For she didn't doubt that Niccolo would want more than one child to continue the D'Alessandro line. Any other woman would have grabbed the offer with both hands, Dani knew. Was she being rash in refusing to marry Niccolo? Was she being fair to their son or daughter by denying its birthright?

She was no longer as sure about that as she had been…

But maybe that had been Niccolo's intent in bringing her here?

Perhaps it was, but being here with him like this, with the magic of Venice and the D'Alessandro palace surrounding them, Dani was finding it more and more difficult to resist the allure…

'Daniella…?' Niccolo prompted again, his expression gently enquiring as he continued to hold his hand out to her.

She gave him a brief smile before stepping forward to take his hand and letting him guide her out onto the balcony. She released herself to step forward and rest both her hands on the railing as she gazed out across the water.

All of Venice lay before her, it seemed. The beautiful

Grand Canal was hazily lovely in the still-warm autumn sunlight as the boats moved continuously along its length, boatmen cheerily greeting each other as they passed. There was an elderly couple in one gondola floating majestically by, their rapt faces telling of their complete enthrallment with their surroundings. Another gondola accommodated a young couple, their arms wrapped about each other and with eyes only for each other.

Dani could see a small child sitting on the balcony of one of the buildings farther down the wide canal. A little girl with dark hair curling silkily onto her shoulders. Her whole attention was on the piece of fruit she was eating with relish, and the sound of her giggle sounded clearly across the water as a young woman, probably her mother, came laughingly out to join her.

And there were so many aromas to assault the senses too. The smell of fresh bread baking. The garlic that was added to most Italian dishes. The juices of many fruits mixed together, adding a freshness to the air that was intoxicating.

Niccolo stood slightly to one side, watching Daniella indulgently as she fell in love with the magic that was Venice.

He had been born here, had lived here all his life, but to him Venice was still a city like no other. A city that twined its tentacles into your heart and never let go. It was easy to see from the glowing fascination on Daniella's face that Venice had already started to take its hold on her heart too; her eyes were glowing mistily, her cheeks were tinged a delicate rose, and her lips slightly parted in wonder.

She shook her head slightly. 'How could Eleni possibly have chosen to leave all this?' she breathed.

'I do not know,' Niccolo murmured as he moved to stand behind her. 'Stay here with me tonight, Daniella,' he said, his hands sliding about her waist as he pulled her gently back to lean against him. 'Please spend the night here with me.' He groaned, lowering his head as he placed lingering kisses against the exposed column of her throat. 'Our child permitting,' he added achingly, 'I would very much like to make love with you in the Venetian moonlight.'

Dani leant weakly against him, her senses having soared the moment his arms moved about her. His lips travelled tantalisingly down the length of her throat, and her hands moved to cover his as they rested against the flatness of her stomach where their child nestled so safely.

'Your child permits,' she assured him throatily. 'As do I...' She turned in his arms to offer her mouth up to the feel, the taste of him as his lips claimed hers.

It was a searching kiss, a seeking, an affirmation that they wanted each other, that their bodies were as perfectly in tune today as they had been on that night four and a half weeks ago, when they had first made love and created a child together.

Dani moaned low in her throat as she felt the heat of her desire for Niccolo in the tingling awareness of her breasts, the nipples having tightened. That heat spread down her stomach, sparking fiercely out of control as it reached between her thighs. She felt Niccolo's own response as his own thighs hardened and his breath caught and became ragged.

Yes, they most definitely still wanted each other!

But...

Niccolo muttered in protest as Daniella gently but firmly moved her mouth away from his to tilt her head back. She looked up at him, the slight pallor to her cheeks telling him that she still had something to say.

Her throat moved convulsively before she spoke. 'Yes, I'll stay here with you tonight, Niccolo.' She nodded, her voice still husky. 'But only if you will promise not to talk of marriage again this evening.' She looked up at him uncertainly.

Niccolo frowned as he gave her a searching look. He could easily read the signs of strain in her expression, the look of almost apprehension—of fear?—in those slightly shadowed green eyes.

But what had she to be frightened of?

He reached up to cradle each side of her face and looked deeply into those troubled green eyes until Daniella deliberately dropped her gaze from his. 'You do know that I would never hurt you, do you not, Daniella?'

'Yes, of course,' she answered quickly.

Too quickly?

She had said she didn't want him to talk of marriage again this evening—would not even contemplate staying here with him until he made such a promise. So could it possibly be marriage itself that she feared? And if it was, what could possibly have happened to Daniella to make her look so fearful at the prospect of marriage? Had her husband hurt her in some way? Perhaps been unfaithful? Was that the reason for the short duration of the marriage?

Niccolo felt a wave of anger deep inside him as he contemplated anyone—most of all Daniella's ex-husband, a man pledged to love and protect her—having hurt her in any way.

But it was an anger he would control until he could return to England and possibly seek out the man Daniella had been married to so briefly; he certainly did not intend to shake their fragile relationship by questioning Daniella about it, either now or in the future.

His thumbs moved caressingly across the paleness of her cheeks as he smiled gently down at her. 'I promise I will not mention marriage again this evening, Daniella,' he repeated teasingly.

Dani looked at him intently, slightly suspicious of the ease with which Niccolo had agreed to her one condition for staying here at the D'Alessandro palace with him tonight.

Not that she doubted he would keep that promise. Niccolo was of all things a man of honour; having made her a promise he would most certainly keep it.

Maybe he was just hoping that their night together, their making love together, would convince her to change her mind?

But it wouldn't.

Would it…?

CHAPTER SEVEN

DANI lay back in the free-standing bath, totally relaxed by the deep warmth of the scented water, its bubbles tickling her chin as she smiled in dreamy contentment.

The luxurious gold fittings and porcelain bathroom suite were unlike anything she had ever seen before, and even this room, she noticed, had a painted ceiling of smiling cherubs. Three of its walls were mirrored, with intricately sculptured surrounds. A bathroom fit for a princess, in fact....

Once they had drunk their tea earlier, Niccolo had suggested that Dani take a nap, and as she was tired from the travelling, as well as the strain of her conversation with him, she had been only too happy to comply. Although she had been shocked by the bedroom Niccolo had told her was for her use—its proportions were immense. In fact, the whole of her apartment in London would probably fit into that one room!

But the beautiful silk-draped four-poster bed had proved to be so comfortable that Dani had fallen asleep in minutes, awaking completely refreshed a couple of hours later.

She hadn't been in the least surprised to find that Niccolo had sent one of his staff to collect her things from her hotel while she was resting. Although it was a little disconcerting to find that someone—probably a maid—had quietly entered the bedroom while Dani was asleep and unpacked the few things she had brought with her.

She had travelled over in tailored black trousers and a green lambswool sweater, but had deliberately brought the formal suit to change into for her interview with Niccolo. However, the delivery of her small overnight case meant that she could now change back into the tailored black trousers and a soft rose-coloured sweater she had intended wearing to travel home tomorrow.

She very much doubted there was going to be any need for formality between herself and Niccolo tonight!

Her heart skipped a beat and her stomach muscles clenched in anticipation as she thought of the night ahead. A night she had told Niccolo she would spend with him.

She felt a quiver of pleasure just at the thought of spending the night in Niccolo's arms. Of making love with him with each of them knowing the identity of the other.

Niccolo had been so wonderful earlier—so warm and caring as he'd solicitously poured a cup of tea for her and then tempted her into eating some of the delicious biscuits that had been on the tea tray. He'd personally showed her into the bedroom, which he'd explained adjoined his, and had made sure that Dani had everything she needed before he'd left her there to sleep.

How easy it was to be lulled into a sense of contentment by such attentions, Dani acknowledged ruefully. How much easier everything would be if she were to just accept Niccolo's marriage proposal and allow him to take charge, relieving her of all the worries of an uncertain future—

She was in love with him, Dani realised with sudden shock as she sat up in the bath.

Not just infatuated by him, as she had been at fourteen. And not just fascinated by him as she had been throughout her teen years. She no longer just suspected that she had loved Niccolo for years; Dani now knew without a doubt that she was totally, utterly in love with Niccolo D'Alessandro.

Dear God…

Her hands shook slightly and she tightly clasped the edges of the bath. She loved Niccolo!

But she had thought she'd loved Philip, too, once, she reminded herself sternly—and quickly followed that with the knowledge that there was absolutely no comparison between what she had felt for the insecure Philip and what she now felt for the self-assured Niccolo.

Maybe not, but she would be a fool—

Dani turned sharply as a knock sounded on the bathroom door. 'Yes…?' she asked tentatively.

The door opened softly and Niccolo stood in the doorway. 'You slept so long I was concerned you might be ill.'

Dani had sunk back beneath the bubbles in the bath as soon as she'd realised someone was actually about to enter the bathroom. Her cheeks burned hotly now that the 'someone' had turned out to be Niccolo. It was more than a little disconcerting to have him come in here like this when she had just discovered she was in love with him.

A discovery she must never, ever allow Niccolo to find out about!

'As you can see, I am perfectly well,' she told him with forced coolness.

He hadn't just been concerned for her physical welfare, Niccolo acknowledged privately to himself. When he had found Daniella's bedroom empty he had briefly thought that she had gone altogether—that she had reconsidered her decision to stay with him tonight and had instead fled the palace.

But then he had seen signs of her presence in the bedroom—a pair of shoes beneath the dressing table, a deep rose-coloured sweater draped on the bedroom chair—and realised that she must be in the adjoining bathroom.

He had spent the hours while Daniella slept in quiet contemplation, knowing that her decision to stay here with him tonight, although positive, did not mean that she would change her mind about marrying him. In fact, the promise she had insisted he make not to pressure her again tonight on the subject implied the opposite.

It went completely against his decisive nature to acquiesce to such a promise, but at the time Niccolo had known he had no choice—that if he didn't make the promise Daniella would not stay.

And he very much wanted her here beside him tonight—wanted to worship and adore her body long into the night, to show her that, although she didn't love him, the physical love between them was beautiful.

As *she* was beautiful, Niccolo thought as he looked hungrily across the room at her. The fire of her hair was secured loosely on top of her head, wispy tendrils curling damply against the slender curve of her neck, and her face was slightly flushed from the heat of the bath water.

A froth of bubbles was hiding her complete nakedness

from him. But that didn't mean that Niccolo couldn't easily envisage the gentle curves of her body: the fullness of her rose-tipped breasts, her slender waist and lithe hips and legs, the dark triangle of auburn hair at the apex of her thighs...

Dani was finding Niccolo's prolonged silence disturbing—especially as she was lying here naked in the bath, while he was fully dressed in a cream silk shirt and tailored brown trousers. And looking disturbingly gorgeous. She groaned inwardly. His overlong dark hair was slightly damp, as if from a shower, and the almost severe handsomeness of his face was dominated by glittering dark eyes as he continued to look at her so intently.

She drew in a ragged breath. 'Was that all, Niccolo?' she prompted pointedly. 'Because my bath water is getting a little cold.'

Instead of leaving, Niccolo stepped farther into the room to collect one of the huge, fluffy cream bath towels from the warming rail before moving to stand beside the bath. 'You must get out before you catch a chill,' he suggested as he shook the towel out invitingly.

Having Niccolo witness her standing up and stepping from the bath was not exactly what Dani'd had in mind when she'd made her pointed comment, intending him to leave.

But it was a little late to feel self-conscious, considering she had already been completely naked in Niccolo's presence the night they made love and that she had agreed to spend tonight with him too. Nevertheless, she did feel shy, and glad of the scented bubbles that still clung to her body as she stood up in the bath, her gaze no longer meeting his as she straightened.

But instead of handing her the towel, as she had expected, Niccolo reached out to wrap the towel around her, draping it over her body beneath her arms before securing the ends between her breasts. His hand briefly lingered there, warm and caressing, his dark gaze steadily holding hers as he stepped back to hold out his hand to her.

'Come,' he said softly. 'It is a very deep bath and I would not like you to trip and fall as you step out.'

Dani didn't want to risk falling either, but the air of intimacy in the room, the sudden awareness she could feel between herself and Niccolo, made her fingers tremble slightly as she placed her hand in his before stepping out onto the deep blue Persian rug.

Niccolo was standing very close, so close he could feel the warmth of Daniella's damp body as his arm lightly brushed against her breast, and he maintained his hold on her hand to look down at her searchingly.

'You're making yourself all wet,' she murmured huskily after a frowning glance at the sleeve of his shirt.

Niccolo would have been happy to make all of his clothing wet just for the chance to hold Daniella in his arms, to kiss her as he had been longing to kiss her again since holding her on the balcony earlier.

But the uneasiness with the situation that he could read in her expressive green eyes warned him to practise caution. Despite the fact that the two of them had made love, that they had created a baby together from that love-making, he knew that Daniella was still shy with him. And he wanted her to feel less, not more self-conscious with him, to give her time to feel at ease with their intimacy.

It took all of his considerable will-power, but somehow

he managed to release her hand and step away. 'I have arranged for us to dine upstairs in the roof garden as it is such a warm evening; I trust that meets with your approval?'

'Oh, yes!' Dani could imagine nothing more magical, her eyes glowing with anticipation as she looked up at him smilingly. No doubt the venue for their evening would make it a very romantic evening too. Which was probably his intention, she thought.

Whoever would have dreamt that the thought of a romantic evening with Niccolo—her adversary for the last ten years—would fill her with such pleasure, such excitement?

Who would ever have predicted she would be about to spend a romantic evening with Niccolo at all?

But she mustn't get carried away here, Dani reminded herself sternly, her smile slowly fading. Niccolo had his own reasons for making this evening as enjoyable for her as possible. And those reasons had nothing to do with romance. Yes, he might have made it more than clear that he wanted to make love with her again. But he had also left her in no doubt that his ultimate objective was to persuade her into marrying him, so that the two of them might share equally in the upbringing of their child.

It didn't matter that Dani had discovered only minutes ago that she was deeply in love with Niccolo; she had to remain on her guard this evening, so as not to be seduced into a false sense of security that might easily persuade her into accepting his proposal. Once tonight was over, Niccolo had to be made to see that she meant it when she said she would never marry again.

'If you wouldn't mind leaving now? I need to go and dress.' She deliberately moved away from him to cross the room and enter the adjoining bedroom, standing in front of the dressing table to study her reflection as she removed the pin from her hair and allowed it to fall down onto her bare shoulders, before picking up her brush and running it through the soft tangles.

She was totally aware of Niccolo following her from the bathroom seconds later. She could see his reflection in the mirror, but she also felt a frisson of physical awareness down the length of her spine that told her of his presence in the room behind her.

Niccolo's gaze was hooded as he studied the slender lines of Daniella's bare shoulders and upper spine, with her hair a tumble of red flame against the silky softness of her skin. He wanted her with a need that was bordering on obsession!

Each time he touched her, spent time with her, Niccolo's need to make love to her again intensified. Getting through the polite ritual of actually eating dinner with her was going to test his control to breaking point.

But it wouldn't break, he decided with determination; too much rested on his not alarming Daniella with the intensity of his need. So instead he forced a teasing smile. 'Can you find your way upstairs to the garden, or would you like me to come back in a short while and escort you?'

'Oh, I think I can find my own way, thank you, Niccolo,' Daniella turned to say lightly.

He gave a curt nod. 'Then I will see you later.'

Dani waited only long enough for Niccolo to leave the bedroom and close the door softly behind him before sinking weakly down onto the chair in front of the dressing table. One glance at her reflection in the mirror showed her that her cheeks were flushed and her eyes glowed deeply green.

It had all seemed so simple earlier, as the two of them stood on the balcony, Niccolo's arms around her and his lips travelling the length of her throat. He had told her that he wanted her to stay with him tonight—had asked her to stay with him, pleaded with her to do so. And as it was what Dani wanted too, she had agreed.

But now, with the prospect of a romantic dinner together followed by a night in Niccolo's bed, Dani was much less sure of the wisdom of accepting such an invitation...

She knew she had been right to have such misgivings when she joined Niccolo in the roof garden half an hour later, to find him sitting at a table beautifully laid with crystal and fine white linen. It was illuminated by several candles floating in a wide water bowl of gold, the only other lighting being several soft amber-coloured lamps that ran the length of the balustrade overlooking the Grand Canal.

Instead of joining Niccolo at the table, Dani moved to stand at that balustrade to gaze out over the breathtaking view that was Venice at night—majestically stunning with the moonlight and softly glowing streetlamps reflected in the water below, several gondolas gliding silently along its length.

Dani was once more so mesmerised, so enchanted, so moved by the beauty spread out before her, that she was incapable of verbally acknowledging Niccolo's presence as he came to stand beside her.

'It is magnificent, is it not?' he murmured.

Magnificent barely described it! No wonder so many couples chose to come here for their honeymoon.

Just the thought of a honeymoon, a natural progression

from the wedding that would have taken place before it, was enough to break Dani out of the spell that Venice— and Niccolo—had been so easily casting over her.

'It's very nice,' she conceded dryly, before deliberately turning her back on the view that was seducing her senses. 'Can we start dinner now? I'm absolutely starving!' She didn't even glance at Niccolo as she moved to the candlelit table and sat down.

Niccolo took his time joining her, his thoughts distracted. Daniella's slightly distant manner told him that she was regretting her agreement to spend the night here with him. That doubt came as no surprise to him, because he had felt those doubts earlier too. But he had no intention, by word or deed, of increasing that uncertainty. He wanted her to enjoy this evening—was even willing to accept that she wouldn't share his bed tonight after all, if that was what she ultimately decided. This was just too important—Daniella herself was too important—to his future happiness for him to ruin it all in one selfish night of need, of desire.

And so he deliberately set out to once more put Daniella at her ease, keeping his conversation light and well away from anything of a remotely emotional nature. Instead, as they ate, he drew her out to talk of her work as an interior designer. The enthusiasm with which she spoke of it, the pleasure in her face, told him of her deep satisfaction in her chosen career—which was one more thing standing in the way of Niccolo's wish that she would eventually agree to marry him and come to live here with him in Venice.

'I am not sure that I believe a woman could ever be that calculating!' he teased, after Daniella broke off telling him a rather amusing story of a woman who had lain on her bed to make sure that she could reach out and adjust her newly installed lighting so that it reflected in the mirrors above and would increase the pleasure for herself and her lover.

'Oh, I can assure you that some of them are,' Dani confirmed, her cheeks colouring bright red as she realised that the single glass of champagne she had allowed herself with her meal seemed to have loosened her tongue. Discussing another couple making love was definitely not something she should be doing with Niccolo, of all people. But despite her earlier nervousness, she had found the evening so relaxing, and Niccolo such easy company, that she had temporarily let her guard down.

Not a good idea when the meal was almost over and the night was rapidly approaching!

'I— This has been a wonderful evening, Niccolo. Thank you,' she told him with stiff politeness.

Niccolo was instantly aware of the return of Daniella's earlier doubts concerning the wisdom of the two of them spending the night together. While he had been totally captivated all evening by how beautiful Daniella looked, by how much he wanted to make love with her again, he'd already vowed to himself that he wouldn't until she was absolutely sure that it was what she wanted, too...

'I assure you, the pleasure has been all mine, Daniella,' he told her honestly.

She gave him a quizzical look. 'I'm curious to know why, when no one else does, you have always insisted on using my full name?'

Yes, he had—and deliberately so. Years ago, when Eleni had been so determined to remain at school in England with her new friend, and Niccolo had been just as determined that she would not, it had been his way of maintaining a disapproving formality between himself and Daniella. In latter years, he recognised ruefully, it had been for another reason entirely...

Niccolo easily held her gaze. 'But I'm *not* the only one who does so, am I?'

Her frown deepened. 'I don't— Oh!' She came to an abrupt halt, no longer relaxed. Her body stiffened. 'You're referring to my grandfather?'

Niccolo had indeed noticed the way in which Daniel Bell always referred to his granddaughter as Daniella when they'd met. He had also been very aware of the way in which the older man almost made it into an insult.

Niccolo reached across the table to cover her clenched hands with one of his own. 'But not for the same reason, Daniella, I do assure you.'

'I'm sorry?' Dani looked across at him uncertainly. The last person she wanted to talk about this evening was her machinating grandfather—although it had certainly brought her back down to earth with a bump!

Niccolo smiled gently at her. 'Unless I am very much mistaken, your grandfather uses your full name as a reminder that, despite being named for him, you are not the grandson he wanted.'

That was very astute of him after just a few hours' acquaintance with her grandfather, Dani thought heavily. It had taken her until she was in her teens to understand that her grandfather was taunting not just herself but her mother, who hadn't produced a male Bell heir. She grimaced. 'And you, Niccolo? Why do *you* insist on calling me Daniella?'

Niccolo could feel the tension in her hands beneath his, and he curled his fingers about them to move his thumb lightly, caressingly, across her tightly clenched knuckles. Her tension was evidence, if Niccolo had needed it, that her grandfather's disappointment that his only grandchild was a girl had been a constant source of hurt to her over the years.

'Because, Daniella, unlike your grandfather,' he said, 'I take total delight in the fact that you are feminine.'

'Oh!' Daniella blinked her surprise at his compliment.

Niccolo felt his inner fury towards Daniel Bell grow in intensity. How dared he cause this beautiful woman—*his* woman, even though she hadn't yet acknowledged it— a moment's pain simply because her gender was not what he had wanted?

'Don't blame my grandfather too much, Niccolo,' Daniella said. 'I'm sure you'll be disappointed, too, if the child I carry should turn out to be a girl and not the male heir you want—need—to carry on the D'Alessandro legacy.'

But Niccolo was an Italian, and to Italian men all children were loved and valued. His own parents, he knew, would have dearly liked more sons to carry on the D'Alessandro name, but after several miscarriages his mother had produced Eleni, thirteen years after Niccolo was born—a child who had been adored by all of them because to them she was a gift from God.

As the child Daniella carried was a treasured gift, regardless of whether it turn out to be a boy or a girl...

'You do not know me well yet, Daniella,' he told her quietly, and he stood up to move around the table to her side, gently pulling her to her feet so that she stood only

inches away from him. 'But never doubt that this child—'
he reached out and placed a hand possessively on the
flatness of her stomach '—*our* child,' he emphasised, 'will
be loved and wanted no matter what its gender.'

Dani's breath caught in her throat, her vision misting
with sudden tears. She knew he meant what he said, and
that he would indeed love their child—perhaps even
already loved their child—whether it was a boy or a girl.
She was grateful for that—knew that it could have turned
out very differently.

Though Niccolo didn't just stop at declaring his love for
their child, she reminded herself heavily. He was insisting
on marrying the mother of his child too. But he didn't love
her, did he?

She stepped away from the warm possessiveness of his
hand on her stomach, able to breathe again once Niccolo
was no longer touching her. 'That's reassuring to know,
Niccolo. Thank you,' she said. 'And I want you to know
that this has been the most romantic evening of my life.'

He regarded her with dark, unfathomable eyes. 'But…?'
he finally prompted.

She quirked her lips. 'How clever of you to know
there's a "but"!'

He gave a humourless smile. 'You have changed your
mind about the two of us sharing a bed tonight, have you not?'

Dani looked at him warily. That was exactly what she
had decided, and she wasn't sure, despite the mildness of
his tone, how he was going to react to being told.

She swallowed hard. 'Are you going to be very angry
if that turns out to be the case?'

Niccolo looked at her searchingly. Daniella expected his

primary emotion to be *anger* that she had doubts about their spending the night together after all?

She turned away to walk over to the balustrade, her back towards him as she spoke. 'Maybe if we had just made love this afternoon instead of waiting...' She stopped and made an attempt to control her ragged breathing. Once she was sure she would be coherent she tried again. 'I've had too much time to think, Niccolo. To realise... It really has been a wonderfully romantic evening.' She turned to face him, her back firmly against the balustrade. 'But now, if you don't mind, I think I would like to go to my own bedroom and sleep alone.' The last was added defensively.

Niccolo studied her beneath hooded lids. 'You say that as if you think I might try to force the issue.'

'Don't be silly, Niccolo!'

But her laugh sounded false to his ears. He was becoming more and more convinced by the second that he was being far from *silly*, as she put it.

He very much doubted that there had been any other man in Daniella's life in the two and a half years since the failure of her marriage... A marriage she had absolutely refused, on several occasions, to discuss with him. If he tried to talk to her about that marriage again now, would he succeed only in alienating her completely? Niccolo had a feeling that he might.

The relationship between the two of them was so very fragile. Too fragile for him to risk even attempting to discuss Daniella's previous marriage with her now. But he made a promise to himself that he would learn the truth about that marriage at the earliest opportunity. Not from

Eleni—because that would not be fair to either his sister or to Daniella. But he would find out the truth somehow.

He moved to Daniella's side, his gaze gently holding hers as he reached out to clasp one of her hands in his before raising it to brush his lips lightly across the softness of her skin. 'Of course I do not mind, Daniella, if that is your wish,' he reassured her gruffly.

Contrarily, a shiver of awareness quivered down Dani's spine as Niccolo's lips touched the back of her hand, and she instantly felt disappointed at Niccolo's easy acquiescence to her request to sleep alone tonight.

Her feelings made no sense whatsoever. Were completely illogical, considering *she* had been the one to say she would prefer not to sleep with him tonight.

But nevertheless, that feeling of disappointment persisted.

'It is,' she told him tersely as she snatched her hand from his grasp and moved sharply away from him. 'I—I'll wish you goodnight, then, Niccolo.' She hesitated at the top of the stairs to look back at him.

'Goodnight, Daniella.' He hadn't moved from where she had left him standing beside the balustrade, the expression in his gaze shadowed in darkness as the candles on the table flickered and died. 'Sleep well,' he murmured.

Dani gave him one last frowning glance before hurrying down the stairs to her bedroom on the next floor.

The bedroom that adjoined Niccolo's.

A fact she became very aware of when, only minutes later, she heard him let himself into the adjoining room.

Dani sat down shakily on her brocade-covered bed, not sure that she was going to be able to sleep at all knowing Niccolo was only on the other side of that connecting door…

CHAPTER EIGHT

'I HAVE brought you morning tea, Daniella.'

Dani roused herself sleepily at the sound of Niccolo's voice, extremely comfortable and warm beneath the bedcovers as she gazed up at him in the semi-darkness of her bedroom.

'I remembered your aversion to coffee yesterday,' he said as he stood beside the bed looking down at her.

'That's very kind of you.' Dani smiled her gratitude.

If she wanted tea or coffee in bed in the morning in London then she had to get up herself and prepare it. And asking any of the staff at the house in Gloucestershire for morning tea or coffee was frowned upon by her grandfather, when they were all perfectly fit and well enough to go down to the breakfast room for it.

She moved to sit up against the downy pillows. The gold brocade curtains were drawn across the huge French doors that led out onto the balcony, shutting out the view, making it impossible for her to tell what time of day it was.

Dani had tossed and turned in the bed for at least an hour the previous evening before falling asleep, and—unusually—she'd had to get up a couple of hours ago in order to be violently ill. She was feeling much better now, even more so after washing her face and brushing her teeth. Obviously this was the start of the dreaded morning sickness!

Still, she felt much better after a couple of hours' more sleep, and the tea sounded very inviting.

'Er—would you care to join me?' she offered as she turned, her eyesight having become accustomed to the semi-darkness, and found that there were two cups on the tray.

'Thank you,' Niccolo accepted, before moving to pick up the chair from in front of the dressing table and setting it down next to the bed. He lowered his long length into it, dressed casually this morning, in faded denims and a black cashmere sweater, his thick hair brushed back from his face.

'What time is it?' Dani asked lightly, in an effort not to feel self-conscious as her cream lace camisole top became visible above the bedclothes as she turned to pour the tea. Pregnant with Niccolo's baby, she would look slightly ridiculous pulling the covers up to her chin like some shy virgin!

'Almost ten o'clock,' Niccolo told her with satisfaction.

'In that case, shouldn't you be at work by now?' Dani frowned as she handed him a cup of tea before picking up her own cup and sipping gratefully. It tasted wonderful!

Niccolo shrugged broad shoulders as he added milk and a spoonful of sugar to his cup. 'I thought the two of us could spend the day together.'

'Oh, but…' Dani shook her head. 'I'm supposed to be flying back to England today,' she said doubtfully.

Niccolo nodded. 'And when you are ready to return to England the D'Alessandro jet will be at your disposal.'

Dani knew all about the family-owned D'Alessandro jet, and remembered teasing Eleni about the sheer luxury of it during their university years, when her friend had made frequent visits home to Venice in it. But Dani had never imagined flying in it herself...

Daniella even looked beautiful first thing in the morning, Niccolo thought distractedly, with her hair fluffed about her face in delicate disarray, her eyes like huge green pools in a face bare of make-up, and the creamy curve of her breasts visible above the low neckline of the lacy camisole she wore. If anything, he wanted her more this morning than he had the previous evening—as the hardening of his body was alerting him all too forcibly!

He shifted restlessly in the narrow confines of the bedroom chair. 'You have a problem with that arrangement?' he asked as he saw her frown.

'Not at all,' she assured him with a husky laugh. 'I was just musing on the luxury of owning your own jet and being able to fly wherever you want, whenever you want.'

'It is the D'Alessandro family that owns its own jet,' he corrected her, with his own frown as he sensed disapproval in her remark.

'Niccolo, as we both know only too well, you *are* the D'Alessandro family!' she teased.

Yes, he was. But he was also Niccolo. And as Niccolo he was becoming increasingly uncomfortable with the physical arousal he felt just looking at Daniella's flushed semi-nakedness.

He was thirty-seven years old, for heaven's sake, and had known many women in his adult life. Yet none of them had ever affected him in the way that Daniella did now just looking at her.

He stood up abruptly—at once realising his mistake as his body instantly betrayed his arousal. He would have to excuse himself. He did not dare risk alarming Daniella with this physical evidence of his desire—

'Niccolo?'

As Dani's eyes became more accustomed to the semi-darkness, the more she was able to discern. And at this moment, as she looked at Niccolo from beneath lowered lashes, she was completely aware of the hard arousal of his body. Her own body answered that arousal and her breasts seemed to swell, the nipples tingling into sudden aware-ness against the softness of her camisole.

Niccolo didn't reply, but he made no effort to disguise the heat that darkened his eyes or the flush against those hard cheekbones as he tightly clenched his jaw.

Dani swallowed hard, knowing that whatever happened next—or didn't happen—it was completely her choice. She knew from Niccolo's gentlemanly behaviour last night that he would not try to initiate anything between them that she didn't absolutely want.

At this moment she knew she wanted him.

Badly!

The reason for her initial sleeplessness last night had been a half-hope, half-dread, that there would be a knock on the communicating door announcing that Niccolo had changed his mind about leaving her to spend the night alone. When the knock hadn't come, Dani hadn't known whether she was relieved or disappointed!

But looking at him now, recognising his arousal, at least

she knew that Niccolo's decision not to come to her last night hadn't been because of any lack of desire on his part.

She turned to carefully place her cup back on the tray beside her. 'Niccolo…?' She held out a hand to him even as she threw back the bedclothes invitingly with the other one. 'Don't question, Niccolo,' she urged as she saw he was about to do exactly that. 'Just come to bed. Please,' she encouraged throatily.

The thrown-back duvet had revealed to Niccolo that Daniella wore French knickers of cream silk and lace to match the camisole top. Her breasts were pert and the nipples hard beneath the silky material, the knickers loose about her slender thighs, and her legs long and silky-soft.

His gaze returned to her face. Her eyes were warm and sultry, her lips—those pouting, full lips that he so longed to kiss—parted in soft invitation.

'Daniella!' He needed no second invitation he moved to join her.

She laughed as she sat up in the bed to swing her feet to the carpeted floor. 'Let's remove some of these clothes first, hmm?' she teased, and she reached out to pull the sweater up his chest and over his head before moving her hands to the fastening on his jeans.

Niccolo stood perfectly still only inches away from her as she unfastened the steel button there, and then the next, and the next, releasing his arousal.

His breath caught in his throat as her delicate fingers moved to touch him there. He groaned low, his eyes closing, as her hand slid beneath his boxers and she began to slowly caress him, fingers curving around him as she moved her thumb along the hard length of his shaft.

Niccolo had lain awake long into the night, unable to stop himself from imagining Daniella touching him like this, caressing him like this, kissing him like this…

Oh, God!

He vividly remembered her heat. Such warm, wet heat. Surrounding him. Drawing him in. Deeper and deeper into that molten fire until it threatened to send him spiralling out of control.

'Let me kiss you, Daniella,' he rasped urgently, and he moved his hands to cup either side of her face, drawing her up into a kneeling position on the bed so that he could claim her parted lips with his own. Their kiss was feverish as Niccolo's tongue plunged deep inside her, licking, tasting, thrusting, claiming that mouth for his own, and his hands ran restlessly down the length of her body to pull her close into his hardness.

As desire and need spun wildly out of control it was almost as if those hours since Niccolo had last kissed her had never happened—although Dani knew that they had, because she had spent most of them fervently wishing he would kiss her again.

Her arms were up about the broadness of Niccolo's shoulders, her fingers threaded into the wild darkness of his hair as she returned the fever of his kiss, and her moan was almost feral as one of his hands moved to cup beneath her breast and he rubbed the pad of his thumb over the already sensitised tip.

Dani's back arched as she moved against that caressing hand, her head dropping back as Niccolo's mouth left hers to travel the length of her throat and down, to capture the other throbbing tip through the thin material of her camisole top with the moist heat of his mouth. He drew it in, suckling fiercely in contrast to the gentle lap of his tongue against the roused hardness of her already engorged nipple.

Dani's fingers clung on to Niccolo's shoulders and her thighs parted as his hand moved the silk material aside to cup her centre, the pad of his palm pressing against her hardened nub as first one finger and then two sought and found her entrance.

Maybe it was because her body already knew the pleasure of Niccolo's, or maybe pregnancy had increased her sensitivity to his caresses, but as Niccolo's fingers continued to stroke inside her, and his lips, mouth and tongue suckled her, Dani felt her body arch anew with the rising force of her imminent release.

'Niccolo...?' Her cry was almost one of bewilderment, and her fingernails dug into the soft flesh of his muscled shoulders.

His hand shifted slightly. The palm was no longer against that hardened nub, but replaced by the caressing pad of his thumb as it moved rhythmically against her, again and again, until Dani could feel the increase in heat, in fire, and she shuddered against his hand in a fierce, pulsating pleasure that seemed as though it would last for ever.

'Oh, God—oh, God!' Her head dropped down weakly onto his shoulder and her mouth moved moistly against him, biting, nibbling in the ecstasies of release.

One of Niccolo's arms supported her back even as he continued to suckle her breast through the now damp material of her camisole. His fingers were stroking, possessing, extorting the last degree of pleasure out of her, and even the briefest caress of his fingers as they left her caused her to quiver in response.

He might not have known the woman he made love with all those weeks ago, but he certainly knew her now! Daniella was a goddess. A goddess of pleasure. Of love. An Aphrodite. And she was his. Every silken, glorious inch of her was *his*.

Niccolo raised his head to look down at her. At the wild tumble of hair about her face and shoulders. At her eyes, dark and slumberous from her recent release.

'You are beautiful, Daniella,' he told her throatily. 'So, so beautiful!' He reached down to swing her up into his arms before laying her down in the centre of the bed, his gaze never leaving hers as he gently slid the damp camisole and French knickers from her body before straightening to remove the last of his own clothing.

Dani gazed her fill of him as she hadn't been able to do the last time they were together, marvelling at the powerful width of his shoulders, his muscled chest, narrow waist and strong, powerful thighs and legs, before her hungry gaze returned to the hardness of his thrusting arousal, long and thick, like tempered steel encased in velvet.

Her gaze returned to his tensely waiting face. 'So are you, Niccolo,' she breathed. 'So are you!' She reached out her arms to him, drawing him warmly against her as he moved to lie down on the bed beside her, and she parted her lips to receive the fierce possession of his.

She could feel the muscles rippling in his back as he half lay across her, his mouth tasting the column of her throat, and she ran her hands down the length of his spine to cup the muscled contours of his buttocks.

Niccolo truly was beautifully male—like the statue of David. Although she thought, from her memory of that particular statue, that Niccolo was better endowed down below than—

My God, what was she *thinking*?

It was impossible to stop the burst of laughter from escaping, although her smile quickly faded as Niccolo raised his head to look down at her with enquiry; it really wasn't the time or place for her to have laughed.

'No, do not stop smiling, Daniella,' Niccolo encouraged as he saw the fading of that smile, the expression in her eyes almost wary now. 'I love to see you smile,' he assured her. 'And lovemaking is not always a serious business, you know,' he added.

She voiced her uncertainty. 'It isn't?'

'Not at all,' he reassured her gently, knowing that once again he had touched upon that area of physical intimacy that Daniella found so—so what?

From the sudden wariness in her eyes just now Niccolo would have said she was almost *afraid* of his reaction to her show of humour—as if she dreaded it might have angered him and feared his response.

He leant on his elbow as he smiled down at her. 'I am reminded of Eleni's reaction after our mother sat her down one day and gave her the "facts of life" talk. I am sure you know the one that I mean…?' He raised mocking brows.

'Oh, yes.' Dani grimaced as she easily recalled the embarrassment she had suffered at having that particular conversation with her own mother. She wondered where he was going with this—he seemed surprisingly relaxed about her laughter just now.

'Exactly.' He nodded. 'Eleni came to me afterwards and assured me that our mother could not possibly be serious about a man wanting to put that part of his body inside her. And that even if he did want to do such a totally gross thing, the woman could not possibly allow him to do it!'

Dani did try to hold back her laughter this time. She really did. But the thought of Eleni saying something like that to her much older and already sexually active brother was just too much for her, and she found herself once again convulsed with laughter.

'I can't believe Eleni really said that to you!' Dani choked once she got her breath back enough to talk at all.

'Oh, yes.' Niccolo lay down on the pillows beside her, one of his arms back behind his head. 'Like you, I found great difficulty in not laughing.'

'What did you say to her?' Dani asked wonderingly.

He shrugged. 'That when the time came she would not find the process quite so gross.' He shook his head. 'I wonder what my little sister would say now if I were to remind her of that talk?' he mused devilishly.

'I wouldn't remind her of it, if I were you.' Dani still grinned as she sat up beside him. 'Although *I* might,' she added mischievously.

Niccolo turned his head to look at Daniella as she sat up on the bed beside him, now totally unselfconscious in her nakedness—as he'd wanted and intended her to be.

He had no doubt now that there was some hidden pain inside Daniella connected with physical intimacy. He was also pretty sure that pain was somehow connected to her ex-husband. Philip Maddox was someone, Niccolo promised himself, with whom he would deal at a later date; it was Daniella who interested him now. And only Daniella.

'May I share your joke now?' he queried gently.

Embarrassed colour darkened her cheeks. 'It wasn't really a joke. I—I was—I was thinking of the statue of David,' she explained uncomfortably. 'About the fact that you—that you're—er…'

'That I am what?' Niccolo encouraged indulgently as Daniella's cheeks flushed anew.

'That you're much better endowed than he is,' she told him awkwardly, before turning her gaze away because she could no longer quite meet his.

'I will take that as a compliment, Daniella.' Niccolo surged up on his elbow beside her, his eyes glowing darkly. 'And that I am so aroused is due entirely to you.'

'It is?'

'Perhaps you would like to discover for yourself just how much I cannot resist you?' he murmured.

'Perhaps I might,' she said teasingly.

Dani hadn't ever imagined that lovemaking could be this much fun—least of all with Niccolo, a man she had only ever seen as either the serious head of the D'Alessandro family or her sarcastic protagonist of the last few years.

But Niccolo's teasing, their mutual laughter, had dispelled any awkwardness she might once have felt at being this intimate with him, and she slid down his body, placing featherlight kisses against his sensitised flesh until she reached her true goal.

'Let's see, shall we?' she whispered as she moved to take him in her mouth, instantly feeling his response as her tongue stroked and her lips caressed.

He felt so good, tasted so good. Her hand gently cupped him as he strained against her, as he groaned low in his throat, and his hands became entangled in the fiery tangle of her hair where it cascaded wildly on the flatness of his stomach.

'Daniella…' he muttered urgently seconds, minutes later, his whole body tensed, his hands clenched into the sheet beneath him.

She made one last stroke with her tongue before relinquishing him reluctantly and looking up at him in the half-light. 'I believe you desire me very much,' she teased, as another light caress of her hand visibly made him arch in a need for release.

'I believe you are right!' he told her fiercely, and he surged up beside her to gently push her back down onto the pillows. He laid claim to her pouting breasts, his hand caressing her before he trailed kisses down her still-flat abdomen to part the silky hair between her thighs and claim her with his lips and tongue.

Within seconds Dani knew that she was on the verge of another climax as Niccolo's tongue flickered against her hardened nub, lapping greedily.

'I want you inside me, Niccolo!' Dani cried achingly. 'I want— Oh…!' Her groan was one of pure pleasure as his tongue suddenly plunged inside her, thrusting rhythmically, taking her to a higher level of pleasure.

Higher.

And then higher still.

Until Dani thought she would disintegrate into a thousand, a million pieces!

'Niccolo, please…!' she whimpered urgently, and her hands moved restlessly against his shoulders. She wanted him inside her, deep, deep inside her, when the explosion came.

Niccolo gentled his stroking tongue before moving slowly, caressingly, back up the lithe length of Daniella's beautiful body, his hardness throbbing wildly for the possession she had just cried out for. 'It will not harm you or the baby if I—?'

'No,' Daniella assured him breathlessly, her eyes feverish, her lips red and swollen. 'The doctor told me it's perfectly safe for me to continue normal sexual relations. But as my "normal sexual relations" at the time were non-existent I— Oh…!' She moaned weakly as Niccolo moved between her thighs to position himself gently against her entrance.

Slowly, oh so slowly, inch by inch, Niccolo entered her, watching the deepening pleasure on Daniella's face even as he kept a tight rein on his control so that he wouldn't just surge deep within her in hard, thrusting possession, stroking rapidly until they both climaxed in wild, mindless ecstasy.

His!

Daniella was his—all his, Niccolo cried silently as he buried himself inside her to the hilt, halting all movement as he gave her time to adjust to his hard length, his jaw clenched in his effort to slow down.

Dani, sensing the sheer effort of will Niccolo was exerting, and knowing his caution was unnecessary, began to move her hips against him, and his own groans of pleasure matched hers as seconds later he rolled over onto his back and took her with him, Dani above him now as he allowed her to take control.

Their gazes were locked as Dani rode him hard and fast, her back arching as Niccolo's hands moved to cup her breasts, as he caressed those fiery tips in that same instinctive rhythm. Then his hands left her breasts to grasp her hips, his expression fierce as he controlled her movements to take Dani with him into a breathtaking, bone-melting climax that raged fierily through every single part of them both.

Dani collapsed weakly down onto him minutes, hours later, to rest the dampness of her forehead against Niccolo's chest, her breathing as raggedly uneven as his own, their bodies still joined.

Niccolo reached up a languid hand to gently caress the fiery length of Daniella's hair as it lay like flame against the darkness of his chest, totally satiated, sure that he had died and gone to heaven in this siren's arms.

He didn't speak—wasn't certain that he could have done so if he had tried!—just held her, sure that a single word would break the spell. And he didn't want this to be over yet. He wanted to just lie here in Daniella's arms, to savour being with her like this. Without any arguments. Without any doubts whatsoever that she belonged to him and always would.

Because she truly was magnificent.

So beautiful. So responsive. So unselfish in her desire to give him as much pleasure as she was feeling herself.

Such lovers, Niccolo knew, were rare—unique.

As Daniella herself was unique.

Niccolo tightened his arms about her, instinctively holding to him what he knew to be his.

What *would* be his!

All he had to do was persuade Daniella into comprehending that too.

All...!

Daniella, as if sensing his fierce feelings of possession, began to stir above him, shifting slightly so that their bodies were no longer joined, before moving to lie down on the bed beside him.

Niccolo instantly turned on his side to face her, knowing by the sudden guarded look in her eyes as she looked at him that she had indeed sensed those feelings inside him and shied away from them.

'Daniella—'

'This changes nothing, Niccolo. You do know that?' Dani cut firmly across his reasonable tone, shaking her head determinedly. 'Physical pleasure is no basis on which to begin a ma—any sort of a relationship,' she amended quickly.

'It is a start,' Niccolo insisted darkly.

'No,' Dani denied.

'Yes, Daniella.'

'No, it isn't, Niccolo,' she repeated quietly, wishing things could be different, but knowing that too much stood between them to ever be overcome just by physical compatibility.

Her brief, disastrous marriage.

The contents of her grandfather's will.

The fact that Niccolo's only reason for wanting to marry her was because she carried his child.

That Niccolo didn't love her as she loved him!

The other things they could maybe have dealt with, given time and understanding, but the thought of loving Niccolo, being in love with him, and knowing that he had only married her out of a sense of Venetian duty and honour would surely destroy any chance of them finding happiness together.

It would certainly destroy *her*.

She could imagine nothing worse than loving Niccolo and being unable to ever tell him how she felt about him— knew that over a period of time, in the close intimacy of a marriage, it would destroy her more utterly than Philip's treatment of her had ever done.

She deliberately averted her gaze from Niccolo's as she moved away from him to sit on the side of the bed. 'I have to shower and dress if I'm to fly back to England today—'

'If *we* are to fly to England today,' Niccolo contradicted harshly, the mattress moving slightly behind Dani as he moved to sit on his side of the bed.

Dani turned sharply to look at him. *'We?'*

He raised dark brows challengingly. 'You did not seriously believe that I would simply let you return to England to face this alone?'

She frowned. 'Face what alone?'

'I believe you said that you have not yet told anyone else about your pregnancy?'

'Yes, that's right. What of it?'

Niccolo shrugged. 'It is my child too.'

'I know whose child it is, Niccolo,' Dani snapped, impatient with the turn this conversation was taking. 'I just don't see—'

'You do not see what, Daniella?' Niccolo's own patience finally snapped and he reached out to grasp her shoulders and shake her slightly. 'Did you really think that I would just remain here in Venice and leave you to face your family alone when you tell them of the child we have made together?' He scowled at her.

In all honesty, Dani hadn't really given much thought to telling anyone else but Niccolo about the baby—had told herself she had to deal with one confrontation at a time.

But Niccolo was right; telling her parents especially was not going to be a pleasant experience. As for her grandfather... The less she thought of her grandfather's self-satisfied reaction, the better!

Niccolo shook her gently again. 'If that really is the sort of man you believe me to be then perhaps you are right, and we do not have a basis on which to build any sort of relationship!' He released her to stand up and collect his clothes from the carpeted floor before crossing the room in measured strides and opening the door that connected to his bedroom. He closed it behind him with barely controlled violence seconds later.

Dani gazed after him in utter misery.

Who would have believed that only minutes ago the two of them had been making love together so beautifully?

CHAPTER NINE

'THERE really is no need for you to come with me to Gloucestershire,' Daniella insisted, for what had to be the tenth time, as Niccolo accompanied her inside her apartment after driving from the private airport where his twelve-seater jet had landed an hour or so ago.

And for the tenth time Niccolo made an effort to control the angry reply he wanted to make!

With nothing left to say between the two of them—as far as Daniella was concerned, that was—Niccolo still had plenty to say on the subject of their marriage—but he had arranged for his pilot to fly them back to England earlier that evening.

His suggestion that they drive down to her parents' home the following day had been quite sensible, it seemed to Niccolo, as Daniella was tired from the hours of travelling and he had some business to attend to in London this evening. But it was a suggestion Daniella was still protesting against most vehemently.

'There is no question of whether or not I will accompany you to Gloucestershire, Daniella,' he bit out forcefully. 'There is only the timing of the visit to decide.'

'I have already decided—'

'You are behaving ridiculously by even considering making that three-hour drive tonight,' Niccolo growled.

Her mouth twisted. 'In *your* opinion.'

Dani knew she was being awkward by insisting on driving to Gloucestershire tonight. Knew it, but couldn't control it.

She was tired and upset, completely over-emotional after hours of travelling with a silently disapproving Niccolo. Not even the luxury of flying in the private jet, with an attentive steward to see to her every need, had helped to alleviate the uncomfortable silence that had existed between herself and Niccolo for all of those hours.

And the same awkward discomfort still existed between them!

It was why she was feeling so contrarily determined not to do what Niccolo wanted her to do and wait until tomorrow to go and visit her parents. Even when she knew he was right. Especially *because* she knew he was right.

'In my considered opinion, yes,' Niccolo said tersely.

'Oh, your *considered* opinion?' she echoed sarcastically. 'Well, that makes all the difference, of course!'

Niccolo drew in an angry breath, knowing that Daniella was spoiling for an argument and that he was determined not to give her one.

She had to know how reckless it would be to make a three-hour drive this evening. It was already growing dark, and she was too tired—as was he—to make the drive safely tonight.

Besides, he really did have some business in London that he simply had to take care of this evening....

'Daniella, please.' He forced a calming tone to his voice. 'Do this for the baby's sake if not for mine, hmm?'

She flinched. 'That was pretty low!'

Niccolo almost ground his teeth with frustration. 'I will use whatever methods I deem necessary in order to make you see sense.'

'Obviously,' she scorned, dropping down into one of the armchairs in her tiny but comfortable sitting room. 'Very well, Niccolo. I will visit my parents tomorrow—'

'No, *we* will visit your parents tomorrow,' he contradicted her harshly. 'Do you have to fight me on everything, Daniella?'

She hadn't fought him this morning. In fact she distinctly remembered being the one to invite Niccolo into her bed!

Which was her main problem, Dani recognised heavily.

Being with Niccolo this morning—making love with him, laughing with him, teasing him during that lovemaking—had only made her fall in love with him even more. And she knew now just how wonderful it could have been between them if things had been different.

If Niccolo had loved her as she loved him.

Something that was never going to happen.

The duty and honour Niccolo offered, his taking responsibility for the child they had created together, had become a bitter taste in her mouth that simply wouldn't go away.

'Yes. I. Do,' she answered him quietly, firmly, knowing that to do anything else but fight the way Niccolo seemed so determined to take over her life was totally unacceptable to her. She could not become some sort of adjunct to Niccolo's life, just the mother of his child, simply because she was too tired or emotional to fight him anymore.

Niccolo sighed. 'I think it's best if I leave you now,' he said wearily. 'I have a meeting later this evening, but I will be staying at Eleni's tonight if you should need me.'

'I won't.'

His mouth tightened at the flat finality of her tone. 'I will be at Eleni's if you should need me,' he repeated, his tone of voice bordering on the savage. 'Tomorrow morning I will drive back here, and then we will go to see your parents together.' He knew he was being overly forceful, knew from the angry glitter in Daniella's eyes that she resented what she saw as his high-handedness, but Niccolo also knew it was either that or he would take hold of her and shake some sense into her.

He had no guarantee of what his next move would be once he touched her again. He had deliberately not touched her since leaving her bedroom this morning. Not even so much as a casual hold on her arm to help her in and out of the jet.

Because he dared not.

He could not be responsible for his own actions once he felt her warm softness beneath his hands. He had never wanted any woman as he wanted Daniella. In every way. Not just physically either. He wanted her laughter, too— and that easy teasing they had found together during their lovemaking. He wanted it all.

But her emotions were so fragile at this moment—*she* was so fragile—that he didn't want to risk saying or doing anything that might shatter their already shaky relationship.

This forced inaction was not an easy thing for a man used to dealing with hundreds of employees on a daily basis, as well as being head of the D'Alessandro family and managing all their finances. It was not an easy thing when dealing with the mother of his unborn child, the woman he—

The woman he *what…*?

Niccolo became very still, his gaze guarded as he looked across at the seated Daniella.

What *was* it he felt for this woman?

Whatever it was he had never felt it before. He was definite about that. He had never wanted to protect a woman as well as cherish her. To make love with her as well as laugh with her. To tell her all of his hopes and dreams as well as his fears.

All of those things he wanted with her.

Yet he knew he could never share his main fear with her—that she would never, ever allow him to have any of the things he wanted with her.

'I will leave you now, Daniella,' he repeated stiffly.

'Fine,' she accepted dully, her head resting back on the chair.

'Daniella, are you all right?'

'What do you want from me, Niccolo?' Her weariness faded as she turned to glare at him with fiercely angry green eyes. 'You've accompanied me to England against my wishes. You're coming to see my parents with me tomorrow, also against my wishes. What else do you want?' she challenged furiously, her hands clenched on the arms of the chair.

Niccolo bit back his reply, instead shaking his head before turning and striding quickly to the door of her apartment before all his good intentions fled and he said or did something he would definitely regret!

Dani watched him leave, angry with Niccolo, but most of all knowing she was angry with herself.

For needing him.

For loving him.

She was less angry the following morning, when Niccolo returned to her apartment to begin the drive to Gloucestershire. Less angry, but more determined.

She had made a mistake yesterday morning by making love with Niccolo. A mistake that would not be repeated. Not that Niccolo looked as if he would care for a repeat of that lapse either. His manner was curt in the extreme as he opened the car door for her to get into the passenger seat, his expression decidedly grim as he settled himself behind the wheel.

She shot him a sideways glance as he manoeuvred the car out into the busy London traffic. Apart from a terse greeting when Dani had answered the door earlier to his knock, Niccolo hadn't even spoken to her this morning.

Had these hours apart given him time to reflect too? To realise that his suggestion that the two of them marry had only been a knee-jerk reaction to knowing that she was pregnant with his child? After careful consideration, had he decided he didn't really want to marry her?

Perhaps it would be better for both of them if Niccolo had decided that.

'You seem a little—preoccupied this morning. Didn't your business meeting last night go as planned?' she ventured lightly.

Niccolo wasn't preoccupied—he was feeling murderous!

But not with Daniella. Never with Daniella.

No, his anger—this almost uncontrollable fury—was directed at another person entirely. But until he had his emotions under tighter control he would have to choose his words carefully.

'I don't remember saying that it was a business meeting, Daniella,' he countered with the same lightness.

'Oh…' Daniella finally murmured, after thinking over his remark for several tense seconds.

It instantly alerted Niccolo to his mistake—so much for choosing his words carefully!

'Neither was it a social occasion,' he assured her. 'It was more in the nature of a—' What the hell could he call his visit last night to Philip Maddox's apartment? A duty call? A need to know the truth about his marriage to Daniella?

Whatever it had started out as, Niccolo had ended up wanting to physically injure the other man. But that would have made Niccolo less of a man in his own eyes, his father having taught him long ago that a man's real strength lay in not resorting to physical violence. So, instead, Niccolo had chosen to rip Philip Maddox apart with words. Hard, cutting words of disgust for a man who had no right to call himself such.

Certainly Philip Maddox would not forget Niccolo's visit in a hurry.

He knew he couldn't talk to Daniella about any of that just yet—that she needed all of her emotional energy at the moment to deal with telling her parents about the baby they were expecting. But later they would talk…

Later Niccolo intended telling Daniella of his visit to her louse of an ex-husband. And he fully intended talking to her again about their own future together.

'It was a meeting that could not be put off any longer,' he concluded.

Which told Dani precisely nothing as to who the meeting had been with or what it had been about!

Perhaps he had no intention of telling her.

Very likely, she acknowledged heavily. Niccolo was a very private person, and had never felt the need to explain himself to anyone, so why on earth should she expect him to be any different with her? She shouldn't, was the answer.

'Sounds a bit boring,' she commented. 'I trust Eleni and Brad are both well?'

Eleni had rung her apartment that morning, but Dani had anticipated such a call from her friend and switched on the answer-machine; her parents first and then Eleni—that was how Dani had decided to deal with this situation. Besides, she had reasoned, if Niccolo wanted to tell his sister about the baby then no doubt he would do so.

'Eleni is intrigued,' Niccolo drawled. 'To quote my little sister exactly, she said, "First Dani disappears for a couple of days and then you turn up— what's going on, Niccolo?"' He gave a rueful grimace.

Dani felt some of her own tension leave her as she easily imagined Eleni's forthright curiosity. 'So what did you decide to tell her?'

He shrugged. 'Nothing. I thought we could join her and Brad for dinner later this evening and tell them our news together.'

Tell them exactly what? That was the question!

Just about the baby? Or did Niccolo also intend confiding in his sister and brother-in-law that he had offered Dani marriage and she had refused?

Eleni would never forgive Dani if Niccolo told her that!

Nothing would please Eleni more, Dani knew, for her

two most favourite people in the world besides Brad to actually marry each other.

Great—now Dani was going to have two lethally determined D'Alessandros to oppose!

Niccolo glanced at Daniella, knowing from her silence that she wasn't altogether happy with his reply. 'I will leave it up to you exactly what we tell them,' he said. 'I realise I am only allowed to be here at all on sufferance!' His voice had hardened with the frustration he still felt at Daniella's stubborn refusal to marry him.

Not that Niccolo intended letting the matter rest there— because, quite simply, he could not do that.

Three and a half weeks ago he had decided he had to give Daniella time to know whether or not she wanted to continue a relationship with him. But now that he had seen her again, spent time with her in his Venetian home, made love with her again, he could no longer bear to be apart from her.

That longing had absolutely nothing to do with the fact that she carried his child. Last night, as he'd lain awake long into the night in one of the guest bedrooms of Eleni's home, his thoughts—all of Daniella—had been enough to convince him of that.

'Perhaps you should tell me exactly how you wish to deal with this when we get to Wiverley Hall?' he asked.

Dani didn't want to 'deal with this' at all! But she appreciated she had no real choice—especially as there had never been any doubt in her own mind that she'd go through with the pregnancy. Not that Niccolo would have given her any choice in the matter; if she had so much as even suggested the possibility of a termination she knew he would have locked her up for the required eight months until she had given birth!

She grimaced. 'I don't intend stopping any longer than it will take to tell my parents about the baby.'

'And your grandfather?'

No, not her grandfather!

Dani had already decided that she simply couldn't bear the look of smug satisfaction that was sure to be on her grandfather's face when he learnt that she was pregnant and hopefully going to give him the great-grandson that he so wanted to continue the Bell name.

'No,' she stated flatly.

Niccolo gave her a brief glance. The look of almost stubborn anger on Daniella's face told him more than any words ever could have done that she had absolutely no interest in how her grandfather reacted to the news of her pregnancy.

'Do you fear that he will once again be disappointed in you?' Niccolo queried gently.

'Disappointed?' Daniella echoed. 'I imagine disappointment is the last emotion my grandfather will feel when he hears he is to be a great-grandfather at last! Or rather that there is to be a Bell heir at last,' she added, with a bitterness that was unmistakable.

That statement, as far as Niccolo was concerned, required clarification! 'Our child will be the *D'Alessandro* heir,' Niccolo reminded her pointedly.

'Not if my grandfather has anything to do with it!' Daniella retorted.

'Which he does not,' Niccolo snapped.

She shrugged, not wanting to carry on this thread of

conversation any longer. 'Then I suggest you take that up with him.'

'Daniella—'

'Look, Niccolo,' she interrupted him. 'You're going to find out later anyway, so I may as well be the one to tell you now…'

'Tell me what?' he prompted guardedly, already knowing from her tone that he was not going to like what he heard.

Dani drew in a ragged breath. She hated having to do this, but knew that if she didn't, then her totally insensitive grandfather was sure to. It was one of the reasons she hadn't wanted Niccolo to accompany her today, if she was honest. Only one of them, of course. But at the moment it was the most urgent.

Niccolo had already questioned the reason for her uncharacteristic behaviour the night of Eleni's party, and once he learnt of that clause in her grandfather's will, he was sure to draw only one conclusion.

An incorrect one, as it happened. But if Eleni, who knew and loved Dani, had felt compelled the day following the party to voice her doubts concerning Dani's motives for making love with Niccolo, how much easier would it be for Niccolo—who didn't know *or* love her!—to have those same doubts?

But it was no good believing—no, hoping—that Niccolo would never learn of that damning threat. As Dani knew only too well, her grandfather had absolutely no conception of the words 'sensitivity' or 'diplomacy', and was only ever interested in his own wants and needs.

It was far better that Dani tell Niccolo the truth now.

Better, but certainly not easier!

CHAPTER TEN

NICCOLO listened in stony silence as Daniella told him of the clause in Daniel Bell's will that could potentially disinherit Beatrice and Jeffrey Bell of not only the Bell money, but Wiverley Hall and the Wiverley Stables, if his granddaughter had not produced an heir before the time of his death.

His hands tightly gripped the steering wheel as he fought to control his inner fury. It was all too easy to guess why Daniella hadn't told him any of this yesterday.

Because she had feared his reaction.

His contempt.

His accusations!

And she was right to do so. His anger and contempt were so strong, so deep, that it was taking every effort of will he possessed not to voice those emotions.

Because he dared not.

Could not.

Not when he was all too aware of the fragility of Daniella's condition.

But that didn't mean there weren't plenty of things he would have liked to say!

'For goodness' sake, say something, Niccolo!' Dani all but shrieked as he remained icily silent.

She knew how bad it sounded—knew how damning it made her actions the night of Eleni's party look. Especially as those actions had resulted in her pregnancy. And she would much rather Niccolo vented his feelings here and now than just sat there in icy silence beside her.

That he was furious there was no doubt. His mouth was a thin line in his tautly set face, his knuckles showing white where his hands were gripping the steering wheel so tightly. He looked as if he would like to hit something or someone—although she knew absolutely that that someone would never be her. Niccolo had far too much honour to ever strike a woman in anger.

At least now she could be assured that Niccolo would never repeat his marriage proposal. Dani had to blink back the sudden hot rush of tears at that realisation. Not that she had believed for one moment that a marriage between the two of them would ever have worked—how could it when she was in love with Niccolo and he felt nothing but a sense of responsibility towards her? But knowing that choice had been firmly taken away from her was enough to make her want to curl up in a ball of misery and cry until there were no more tears left. About forty or fifty years should do it!

Niccolo drew in a harsh breath. 'I am not speaking because—' He broke off abruptly. 'Daniella, I think it is better if I say nothing at all on this subject until we can be alone somewhere more—suitable for such a conversation.'

The fact that Niccolo couldn't even talk about it right now was enough to tell Dani just how deeply angry he felt.

But what else had she expected? That Niccolo would agree her grandfather's demands were totally unreasonable as well as selfish? That Niccolo wouldn't view Dani's own actions on the night of Eleni's party as a deliberate ploy on her part to provide her grandfather with the heir he demanded?

Fat chance!

'Yes. Of course,' she agreed quietly, her throat actually aching from the effort of trying to suppress her tears. 'I'm sorry, Niccolo,' she added gruffly.

'You—' He broke off his explosion, his knuckles having turned even whiter. 'We will talk later, Daniella,' he said instead.

What was left for the two of them to talk about Dani had no idea. Although she was pretty sure the question of with which one of them the baby's future lay would come into that discussion somewhere….

'I'm very tired, Niccolo, so I think I'll take a nap, if you don't mind,' she told him wearily, and she rested her head back against the car seat and closed her eyes.

Niccolo glanced at her briefly, his mouth tightening as he noted her pallor and the dark circles beneath her closed lids, before determinedly turning his attention back to the road ahead. To allow his tumultuous thoughts full rein would only distract him from driving and so put both their lives in danger. Something he had no intention of doing.

There would be plenty of occasions for acting upon his thoughts once they reached Wiverley Hall!

Dani, as an only child, had always been very close to her parents, and telling them of her pregnancy when she wasn't married to the baby's father—or even intending to be—was probably the hardest thing she would ever have to do in her life.

Thankfully, she and Niccolo arrived an hour before lunch. Her parents would be in the sitting room together, talking over their respective morning activities before it was time to eat. Her grandfather, Dani knew, would have gone out for his late-morning constitutional, but he would be back in time for lunch, so this respite alone with her parents was limited.

'What a lovely surprise, darling!' Her mother stood up to hug her warmly, an older version of Dani herself, with her rich red hair and warm hazel eyes.

'Why didn't you let us know you were coming?' Her father gave her a brief, quizzical look as he received his own hug before turning his attention to their guest. 'Mr D'Alessandro—it's good to see you again.' He shook the younger man warmly by the hand.

'Daniella wanted to surprise you both,' Niccolo answered smoothly when it became obvious Daniella was at a loss as to how to begin telling her parents of the reason for their visit.

'Well, she succeeded.' Jeffrey Bell, a tall, thin, slightly weathered-looking man, after hours of working outdoors with his horses, with blond hair liberally streaked with grey and eyes of twinkling green, gave his daughter an indulgent smile before indicating they should all sit down in the comfortably worn chairs in the family's informal sitting room.

Niccolo waited until Daniella had seated herself on the edge of the faded gold-coloured sofa before deliberately sitting down next to her, and taking one of her hands firmly into his.

Daniella gave him a nervous glance, but left her hand where it was, her fingers curling slightly about his, as if drawing strength from this physical contact.

As she was meant to do. Niccolo's own parents were no longer alive, but he could still imagine the ordeal it must be for Daniella to come here today and tell her parents of her pregnancy. But whatever other circumstances had prevailed, Daniella had not become pregnant on her own, and the responsibility for this announcement was as much his as it was hers.

He knew by the way Daniella's throat moved convulsively that she was having serious trouble finding the right words with which to begin. He turned to the older couple. 'Daniella and I have something we wish to tell you both—'

'Well, isn't this cosy?' The loud voice of Daniel Bell interrupted suspiciously.

Niccolo stood up slowly to turn and stare coldly at the elderly man where he stood in the doorway, looking at them all with shrewd green eyes. The same green eyes that in his granddaughter were warm and gently loving.

'Major Bell,' he bit out in icy recognition, before turning back to Daniella as she still sat frozen into immobility on the sofa, her guarded gaze fixed on her grandfather. 'Will you forgive me, *cara*—' Niccolo spoke to her gruffly '—if I take your grandfather away for a few minutes?'

Dani raised startled eyes to look at Niccolo. Why on earth—?

'I will not be long, I promise.' Niccolo gave her a gently encouraging smile.

'I— Of course.' She nodded, at the same time blinking her eyes in confusion at this development.

Was Niccolo—aware from their earlier discussion that she did not want her grandfather present during this conversation—just giving her some privacy in which to talk to her parents? Or did he have some other reason for spiriting her grandfather away? Whatever Niccolo's reasoning, Dani could only feel relief at his giving her these few minutes alone with her parents.

'Thank you.' She gave Niccolo's hand a grateful squeeze.

'You are more than welcome, *cara*,' he assured her, and he raised her hand, his gaze intent on hers as he placed the lightest kiss against the back of that hand before releasing her and turning back to her grandfather. 'Major Bell, I wish a few minutes' private conversation with you, if you would be so kind?' It was voiced as a question, but the hard determination of Niccolo's tone brooked no argument against the request.

Dani had been slightly thrown by Niccolo's endearment, and that kiss on the back of her hand, but nevertheless she saw the surprise that widened her grandfather's eyes at the younger man's tone before he brought the emotion under control.

He looked at Niccolo with mocking enquiry. 'Well, of course, D'Alessandro,' he drawled confidently. 'We can go to my study.' He stepped back to allow Niccolo to precede him out of the room, a move Niccolo deftly avoided as he stood aside deferentially to allow the older man to lead the way.

Dani's breath left her in a whoosh of relief once the two men had left the room—an emotion echoed by her parents, if their weary sighs were anything to go by. Although the fact that Niccolo and her grandfather had gone now meant that Dani had to tell her parents about the baby by herself before the two men returned—something that was proving a lot harder than she had imagined.

After all, she was twenty-four years old, and ran her own successful business in London; it wasn't as if even without Niccolo's emotional support she couldn't keep herself and her unborn baby. But it wasn't really about that. Her parents, as Dani knew only too well, had been deeply distressed for her when her first marriage had ended in the way that it had. In fact, it had taken all of her persuasion at the time to talk her father out of going to London to confront Philip and tell him exactly what he thought of him!

And now Dani was about to tell them that their only daughter was going to be an unmarried mother in around eight months' time!

It was—

All three of them turned towards the door in alarm as the sound of Daniel Bell's shouting could clearly be heard all the way down the length of the hallway that led to his study!

Dani rose unsteadily to her feet. 'What...?'

Her parents seemed frozen in their chairs. Her father was the first to recover enough to speak ruefully. 'Exactly what did Mr D'Alessandro want to talk to your grandfather about?' he murmured.

There were a few seconds' silence, as Niccolo obviously replied softly to the older man, followed by yet more shouting from Dani's grandfather.

'I have no idea!' she replied.

If Niccolo had told her grandfather about the baby then anger was the last reaction Dani would have expected. But if Niccolo was discussing anything else with her grandfather then she really didn't have a clue what it could be.

She certainly intended finding out!

'I don't think that's a good idea, Dani.' Her father reached out to grasp her arm as she would have hurried from the room to go to her grandfather's study. 'Mr D'Alessandro strikes me as the sort of man who can take care of himself,' he told her. 'And anyone else who comes along, hmm?' he added softly.

Dani turned back to her father, and the gentle questioning in his eyes was almost her undoing. It *would* have been her undoing if at that moment she hadn't heard the door to her grandfather's study being opened and then closed again with studied force, followed by the sound of someone walking down the carpeted hallway.

Who—?

A grimly satisfied Niccolo entered the room. 'Major Bell has decided not to join us, after all,' he announced.

There was complete silence in the room, and then Jeffrey burst into appreciative laughter. 'I have no idea what you said to my father, Niccolo, but anyone who can best him in an argument—I take it you *did* best him?' He waited for Niccolo's nod before continuing. 'Then you deserve a medal!' he exclaimed, and he crossed the room to slap the younger man on the back.

Jeffrey Bell's lack of rancour on his father's behalf came as no surprise to Niccolo now that he understood the overbearing way in which Daniel Bell had ruled this household for the last twenty-five years. It was the total look of bewilderment on Daniella's face that concerned him at this moment.

He crossed swiftly to her side. 'I assure you that your grandfather is perfectly well. He is merely sulking in his study,' he said dryly.

Sulking?

Her grandfather was *sulking*?

Surely only young children who couldn't have their own way did that?

Then Dani realised that was exactly how her grandfather behaved like: a spoilt and petulant child who always wanted his own way. The only tried and tested way to deal with a spoilt and petulant child was to deny them what they wanted—and Dani knew only too well what her grandfather wanted most!

'Exactly what did you say to him, Niccolo?' Dani wanted to know.

He shrugged. 'The truth.'

She frowned. 'About...?'

'Perhaps I should have said that I told your grandfather a few home truths,' Niccolo amended.

Dani swallowed hard. 'Such as?'

Niccolo looked at her searchingly, easily able to see the strain in her face as she looked up at him anxiously.

He turned to look at her parents. 'I wonder, Beatrice and Jeffrey, if you would mind allowing me a few minutes alone with Daniella? We have some very exciting news to share with you both, but I believe I first need to—to talk to your daughter.'

'Niccolo—'

He reached out and once again took her hand in his. 'We could have this conversation in front of your parents, if that is your wish. But I believe they may find it a little embarrassing to witness me going down on one knee while I propose to you!'

She shook her head. 'I've already told you that I won't—'

'*Cara,*' Niccolo silenced her gently, lifting her hand to brush his lips against her softly scented skin, his gaze intent upon hers. 'It occurred to me, while you were asleep on the drive down here, that when we talked yesterday I somehow failed to propose properly to you. With your permission, it is an omission I intend correcting before we talk to your parents.'

Dani was still rather dazed. Niccolo didn't need her 'permission' to do anything. Neither could she see what difference his *asking* her to marry him rather than telling her was going to make.

'I think it's best if we do leave you two alone for a while,' her mother told her gently as she came over to squeeze her arm understandingly. 'Daddy and I will just go through to the kitchen and tell Cook there will be two more for lunch.'

'But I believe we'll leave Father to sulk for a while longer,' Dani's father added.

'That arrangement sounds perfect.' Niccolo was the one to agree.

'I thought it might.' Jeffrey laughed. 'Don't keep us waiting too long for this news of yours, hmm?' he added warmly.

Dani waited until her parents had left the sitting room before turning back to Niccolo. 'I'm sorry, Niccolo, but don't think you getting down on one knee and proposing is going to make the slightest difference to what my answer has to be.'

'*Has* to be?' he echoed softly, his head tilted slightly as he looked down at her.

Dani removed her hand from Niccolo's clasp before moving away, totally unnerved by his close proximity. 'I simply can't marry you, Niccolo—'

'Why not?'

'Because I *can't*!' she groaned.

So much for her earlier certainty that Niccolo would never repeat his offer of marriage!

But to be married to Niccolo, loving him, *in* love with him, when he didn't return those feelings, had to be her idea of hell on earth….

'It wouldn't work, Niccolo—'

'Everything works between us, Daniella,' he cut in softly.

She gave a weak smile. 'You're talking about sex, Niccolo—'

'I'm talking about making love,' he corrected. 'And we do make love, Daniella.' His voice lowered to a sensuous murmur that made Dani shiver. 'Even that first time we made beautiful love together. Deny it if you can.'

Dani couldn't. She already knew that what she and Niccolo shared physically was exceptional. Perfect.

She shook her head. 'I'm not going to deny it, Niccolo.' She sighed. 'But what happens when I'm huge with our child and no longer sexually attractive? If we were married would I be expected to just sit by while you went out and found yourself a mistress—?'

'No!' Niccolo exclaimed, frowning darkly at the mere

thought of ever making love to any other woman but Daniella. 'No,' he repeated gently as he crossed the room to her side. 'Daniella, perhaps our…courtship has been a little brief. Certainly the nature of it has been reversed, in as much as we made love first and then afterwards got to know each other—and are still learning about each other,' he acknowledged ruefully. 'But I do not just want you in a sexual way, Daniella. I want all of you.'

She looked up at him, heartbreakingly earnest. 'What does that mean?'

He smiled. 'It means that I know you are not in love with me yet, but that I hope, given time, to persuade you into loving me as much as I love you. And I *do* love you— a great deal, Daniella,' he added throatily. 'I love you as I never thought I would love anyone,' he told her intently. 'I love you more than life itself!'

Dani stared at him, completely dumbstruck, completely overwhelmed! 'I— But— You can't love me!' she finally managed to gasp.

Niccolo's smile deepened. 'The fact that you are the only person I know who would dare to tell me who I can or cannot love is one of the reasons that I do love you.'

'But—but you never even approved of me as a friend for Eleni.'

'I was guilty of that arrogance, yes.'

'And even less so after my marriage and divorce,' she continued, frowning now.

He drew in a sharp breath. 'You are in no way responsible for the brevity of your marriage to Philip Maddox!' he told her harshly.

Dani looked up at him cautiously, seeing the fierce

anger in his gaze. And yet it was an anger she was some-how sure was not directed at her....

What did Niccolo know of her marriage to Philip? How did he know? Surely Eleni couldn't have told him?

'The meeting I told you I had in London yesterday evening was with Philip Maddox,' Niccolo continued, his eyes narrowed intently as he recalled that meeting.

'You went to see Philip?' Daniella gaped.

'I certainly did. And I cannot believe that any man could have treated you in that way. He was your husband, and had only just promised before God to love and protect you!'

He shook his head in disgust as he thought of his con-versation the evening before with Daniella's ex-husband. The sorry excuse for a man had admitted that, in a fit of uncontrollable jealous rage, he had all but raped his own wife on their wedding night.

Niccolo had already guessed that it had to be something as awful as that after sensing Daniella's aversion to even the idea of marriage. A few minutes' conversation with Philip Maddox had confirmed his own worst fears.

He looked at Daniella with concern now as she moved to one of the chairs to sit down heavily, her face very pale. 'I don't understand. What made you go and see Philip in the first place?'

'You did, *cara mia*,' Niccolo confirmed as he went down on his haunches beside her chair, his gaze intent on hers. 'These last two days in Venice, you several times looked at me warily, almost with fear, when you thought you might have angered or displeased me, as if you were frightened of what my reaction might be. But please believe me when I tell you I would never force you to do anything you did not want to do, Daniella.'

She already knew that!

Just as she knew—had always known—that Niccolo was nothing like Philip. Niccolo was strong where Philip was weak. Niccolo was honourable where Philip was selfish. Niccolo would never use physical force on any woman. Because Niccolo was—well, *Niccolo*!

The man she loved.

Enough to marry him? Enough to forget the aversion to the commitment of marriage that Philip had so forcefully instilled in her? Enough to entrust her love, the rest of her life, into Niccolo's hands?

God, yes!

Loving Niccolo and knowing that he loved her in return, wiped away any doubts she might have had about marrying again. Because, she realised wonderingly, loving Niccolo, knowing that he loved her, made her strong, not vulnerable.

Niccolo clasped one of her hands tightly in his. 'I will never allow anyone to harm you ever again, Daniella,' he vowed passionately. 'Not Philip Maddox. And certainly not your grandfather,' he added grimly.

Dani felt some of the tension of the last few minutes leave her as she looked ruefully at Niccolo. 'What *did* you say to him just now?' she asked.

Niccolo shrugged. 'I merely explained that I was thinking of setting up my own stables and going into the horse-training business, and that Jeffrey would be the perfect partner for that business. A move that would, of course, necessitate Beatrice and Jeffrey moving from Wiverley Hall to the more modern facilities I intend purchasing. I explained how sorry I was that this would mean he would lose his unpaid housekeeper as well as a source of income, but that I believed the move to be necessary for the happiness of my future wife.'

'It is,' Dani assured him happily.

'I also informed him, without telling him that you are already pregnant, that it is our intention for any children you may or may not have in the future to be D'Alessandros and not Bells. It *is* our intention, is it not…?' Niccolo prompted, suddenly touchingly uncertain.

'It most definitely is,' she breathed shakily, her fingers tightening about his. 'But—Niccolo, earlier in the car, when I told you about my grandfather's will, I thought you were angry with me because you believed I had deliberately set out to become pregnant by you.'

'The anger I felt at that time was directed solely towards your grandfather, for threatening you and your parents in this despotic manner,' he corrected with an impatient shake of his head 'No man has the right—and especially not a father and a grandfather—to use emotional and financial blackmail in that way.' He raised one dark eyebrow. 'If it is any consolation, I do not believe, once your grandfather has thought the situation through, that he will carry out any of his threats.'

Dani had a feeling that Niccolo would turn out to be right—that her grandfather really had no wish to end up alone and lonely at Wiverley Hall.

Just as she appreciated that it was Niccolo, in his desire to protect her and all she loved, who had made all this possible…

Because he loved her.

Niccolo *loved* her!

She swallowed hard. 'You can go down on one knee and propose now, Niccolo,' she encouraged throatily.

Niccolo looked at her intently and saw the slight flush on her cheeks, the smiling curve to her lips, the warm glow in her eyes.

He moved down onto one knee, her hand held tightly in his. 'Daniella, I love you. I will always love you, and only you, with all of my heart. You are the woman I adore, the body I worship—that I will desire even when you are big with our child,' he added teasingly. 'Will you please marry me and so make me the happiest of men?'

Dani heard every wonderful word of his proposal, cherished every syllable. 'Niccolo,' she began shakily, 'I love you. I will always love you, and only you, with all of my heart. You are the man I adore…' her voice strengthened as she echoed his words '…the body I worship—that I will desire even when I am big with our child,' she added ruefully. 'Yes, I will marry you—and gladly make you the happiest of men, as it will make me the happiest of women to be your wife!'

'Daniella…' Niccolo groaned even as he reached up to take her in his arms and claim the warm invitation of her lips with his own.

She was finally his!

And she would remain his for all time, to be loved and adored as she so deserved to be loved and adored. And he knew Daniella would love and adore him in return.

Niccolo asked for no greater happiness….

EPILOGUE

THEY were married only three weeks later, in a wedding—
despite the speed with which it had been organised—that
was every bit as beautiful as Eleni's had been the previous
year.

All of the D'Alessandro family was present, with Eleni
herself beaming proudly at Dani and Niccolo throughout
the service as she watched her beloved older brother marry
her beloved best friend.

All the Bell family were there too. Dani's happily proud
parents. Her grandfather too. Even if he was a little more
subdued these days than he'd used to be.

But Dani had no doubt that he would soon bounce back
to his normal obnoxious self. Once he got over the fact that
his new grandson-in-law could buy him out a hundred
times over, and was a man who wouldn't allow anyone to
bully or threaten the people he loved—namely Dani and
her parents.

And during the months following the wedding, after
Dani moved to Venice to live with Niccolo and the two of
them eagerly anticipated the birth of their child, Dani knew
herself to be very much loved and adored. Their love for

each other became deeper and stronger as the two of them came to know each other more intimately.

Seven months later Niccolo cried unashamed tears of pride and happiness, with Dani's hand tightly clenched in his, when their daughter, Sofia Beatrice D'Alessandro, entered the world and claimed their hearts.

A child created by their love.

A cherished and beloved daughter who would one day be joined by two younger brothers: Daniele Niccolo D'Alessandro and Pietro Cesare D'Alessandro.

The D'Alessandro heirs....

Turn the page for an exclusive extract
from Harlequin Presents®
RAFFAELE: TAMING HIS TEMPESTUOUS VIRGIN
by
Sandra Marton

"IN THAT CASE," Don Cordiano said, "I give my daughter's hand to my faithful second in command, Antonio Giglio."

At last, the woman's head came up. "No," she whispered. "No," she said again, and the cry grew, gained strength, until she was shrieking it. "No! No! No!"

Rafe stared at her. No wonder she'd sounded familiar. Those wide, violet eyes. The small, straight nose. The sculpted cheekbones, the lush, rosy mouth...

"Wait a minute," Rafe said, "just wait one damned minute...."

Chiara swung toward him. The American knew. Not that it mattered. She was trapped. Trapped! Giglio was an enormous blob of flesh; he had wet-looking red lips and his face was always sweaty. But it was his eyes that made her shudder, and he had taken to watching her with a boldness that was terrifying. She had to do something....

Desperate, she wrenched her hand from her father's.

"I will tell you the truth, Papa. You cannot give me to Giglio. You see—you see, the American and I have already met."

"You're damned right we have," Rafe said furiously.

"On the road coming here. Your daughter stepped out of the trees and—"

"I only meant to greet him. As a gesture of—of goodwill." She swallowed hard. Her eyes met Rafe's and a long-forgotten memory swept through him: being caught in a firefight in some miserable hellhole of a country when a terrified cat, eyes wild with fear, had suddenly, inexplicably run into the middle of it. "But—but he—he took advantage."

Rafe strode toward her. "Try telling your old man what really happened!"

"What *really* happened," she said in a shaky whisper, "is that…is that right there, in his car—right there, Papa, Signor Orsini tried to seduce me!"

Giglio cursed. Don Cordiano roared. Rafe would have said, "You're crazy, all of you," but Chiara Cordiano's dark lashes fluttered and she fainted, straight into his arms.

* * * * *

Be sure to look for
RAFFAELE: TAMING HIS TEMPESTUOUS VIRGIN
by Sandra Marton
available November 2009 from Harlequin Presents®!

HARLEQUIN *Presents*

EXTRA

SNOW, SATIN AND SEDUCTION

Unwrapped by the Billionaire!

It's nearly Christmas and four billionaires are looking
for the perfect gift to unwrap—a virgin perhaps,
or a convenient wife?

One thing's for sure, when the snow is falling outside,
these billionaires will be keeping warm inside,
between their satin sheets.

**Collect all of these wonderful festive titles
in November from the Presents EXTRA line!**

The Millionaire's Christmas Wife #77
by HELEN BROOKS

The Christmas Love-Child #78
by JENNIE LUCAS

Royal Baby, Forbidden Marriage #79
by KATE HEWITT

**Bedded at the
Billionaire's Convenience #80**
by CATHY WILLIAMS

HARLEQUIN *Presents*

kept for his
Pleasure

She's his mistress on demand—but when
he wants her body and soul, he will be
demanding a whole lot more!
Dare we say it…even marriage!

PLAYBOY BOSS,
LIVE-IN MISTRESS
by *Kelly Hunter*

Playboy Alexander always gets what he wants…
and he wants his personal assistant Sienna as his
mistress! Forced into close confinement, Sienna
realizes Alex isn't a man to take no for an answer….

Book #2873
Available November 2009

Look for more of these hot stories throughout the year
from Harlequin Presents!

www.eHarlequin.com

HP12873

HARLEQUIN *Presents*

TWO CROWNS, TWO ISLANDS, ONE LEGACY

A royal family torn apart by pride and its lust for power, reunited by purity and passion

THE ROYAL HOUSE *of* KAREDES

Look for the next passionate adventure in
The Royal House of Karedes:

THE GREEK BILLIONAIRE'S INNOCENT PRINCESS
by Chantelle Shaw, November 2009

THE FUTURE KING'S LOVE-CHILD
by Melanie Milburne, December 2009

RUTHLESS BOSS, ROYAL MISTRESS
by Natalie Anderson, January 2010

THE DESERT KING'S HOUSEKEEPER BRIDE
by Carol Marinelli, February 2010

www.eHarlequin.com

HP12867

HARLEQUIN
Ambassadors

Want to share your passion for reading Harlequin® Books?

Become a Harlequin Ambassador!

Harlequin Ambassadors are a group of passionate and well-connected readers who are willing to share their joy of reading Harlequin® books with family and friends.

You'll be sent all the tools you need to spark great conversation, including free books!

All we ask is that you share the romance with your friends and family!

You'll also be invited to have a say in new book ideas and exchange opinions with women just like you!

To see if you qualify* to be a Harlequin Ambassador, please visit www.HarlequinAmbassadors.com.

Thank you for your participation.

BAP09BPA

REQUEST YOUR FREE BOOKS!

HARLEQUIN *Presents*

PASSION
GUARANTEED
SEDUCTION

2 FREE NOVELS PLUS 2 FREE GIFTS!

I ♥ HARLEQUIN® *Presents*

BROUGHT TO YOU BY FANS OF HARLEQUIN PRESENTS.

> We are its editors and authors and biggest fans—and we'd love to hear from YOU!

Subscribe today to our online blog at
www.iheartpresents.com